Paris of the Pacific Northwest

Eleven Stories and a Play

Kempton Dexter

Joy Wood.
Happy Days
K. Dexter
2021

◆ FriesenPress

Suite 300 - 990 Fort St
Victoria, BC, V8V 3K2
Canada

www.friesenpress.com

Straw Hat Publishers
119 885 Dunsmuir Rd.
Victoria BC V9A 6W6
Cover Art: Sandy with Child
Editor: Lon Littleford

ISBN
978-1-5255-9200-3 (Hardcover)
978-1-5255-9199-0 (Paperback)
978-1-5255-9201-0 (eBook)

1. FICTION, SHORT STORIES (SINGLE AUTHOR)

Distributed to the trade by The Ingram Book Company

Contents

Margaret

Gillian Margaret Simpson went into her son's bedroom and gathered up his bedding for the laundry. She tried not to indulge in the sheets revealing evidence of his sex life. Her sweet and funny little boy had turned into a gangly masturbation machine. Fourteen years of parenting had taught her that one must take change in stride. Still, this recent transformation into reproductive animal touched her deeply. The feelings cut a wide swath, from sad and threatened, to pride and a sense of reckless invulnerability. She knew she had an overly active imagination and apparently her son did as well.

The image of frozen laundry hanging stiff on a clothesline in the dead of winter came to mind. She sighed, then smiled and shook her head. Margaret held a nagging curiosity but wasn't wanting to acknowledge what that curiosity was about. Then it dawned on her. What was the object of his desire? What or who did he think about while spreading his seed? Was that any of her business? Of course it was, sort of.

He wasn't allowed to have a computer in his room and Margaret hadn't stumbled across any girly magazines. He probably just fantasized about the girls at school, or at least, she assumed it was girls. He was a sensitive young man.

Sensitive like his father had been and her father too. Both of them were full-time working lads at her son's age. They were men at fourteen, so was the boy, in body at least.

She put the soiled laundry in her basket and walked out of the bedroom into the hallway. There was a window near the top of the stairs and she paused to look outside. The snow on the ground was in blotches. The frozen earth was exposed where it saw enough of the limited winter sun. The barn still had a sizable snowdrift, a weary white wave paying homage to the barn's north facing wall.

Her hazel coloured eyes scanned the dull white sky. It was growing cold again and a few snowflakes were wiggling their way downward. At the edge of the field stood the horizon line of black spruce, tall hemlock and a tangle of grey deciduous limbs. Their definition faded in and out of focus beyond the meandering wedding veil of falling snowflakes. Margaret fussed with the gold band on her ring finger as she searched the fading landscape.

Suddenly, she put her basket down and returned to her son's room. Carefully, she began to search. It was a small room and before long she realized there was no evidence of any pornographic material. The mother sat on the unmade bed, then lay on it. The ceiling was like a still photo of what she had seen looking out the hallway window. She closed her eyes, considering what the boy pictured against the blank slate.

It came instantly. It was Sonya, the neighbour girl who was a year older than her Grant. The young woman had a pin-up figure and the teenage wardrobe to exploit it. Those snug little sweaters would no doubt instill a life long breast fetish in her darling little innocent boy.

6

Margaret rolled over on her side. The absurdity of this exercise caused her to volunteer, "Oh, god." Besides she had plenty to do. There were two on-line students to tutor. One in French, the other in German. Why would a thirty-two year old Korean architecture student want to learn German? There were plenty of reasons, no doubt.

She looked at her wrist watch. 11:13a.m. She had plenty of time. Tutoring college students in language was her bread and butter. Her son may have inherited her vivid imagination but he had completely missed her facility for languages. Genetics was a fickle mistress.

Margaret looked over the edge of the bed and then stretched until her head was upside down, peering under the bed. The was a book.

"The Oxford dictionary of Current English," she said, picking it up she laying on her back again. The dictionary was bookmarked with a large sheet of writing paper and she opened it. Her son had written out one complete entry of one of the book's 25000 plus words. Margaret read slowly.

"Dead. Adjective, no longer alive. Colloquial, extremely tired or unwell. Having lost sensation. My fingers are dead. With to, unappreciative of, insensitive to. No longer effective or in use, extinct. Dead as a dodo. Distinguished or inactive. Dead match, dead volcano. Inanimate, lacking in vigour, dull, lustreless, not resonant, no longer effervescent. No longer effervescent."

"Interesting."

Margaret held the dictionary to her flat chest and wondered why her son had written out this definition word for word. Then she thought about how the book would lie on Sonya's chest.

"Indeed a distinguishable contrast," she said to the ceiling. Margaret continued.

"Quiet, lacking activity. Not transmitting sound. Radio's dead. Ball games, out of play. Abrupt, complete, exact, unqualified. Dead stop, dead calm, dead centre, dead certainty. Adverb, Absolutely, extremely, completely, exactly. Dead right, dead tired, dead against, dead on target."

Margaret raised her eyes, thinking she heard an unusual sound. She stood, went into the hall and looked out the window. Nothing, except the veil of snow was thickening. She returned to the bed, laid on her back, and continued to read aloud.

"The dead. Dead person, all who have died. Cut person dead, deliberately ignore his presence. Dead beat, exhausted. Dead-beat, penniless person. Dead duck, unsuccessful or useless person or things. Dead end, closed end of passage, course offering no prospects. Dead hand, oppressive posthumous control. Dead head, faded flower head, non-paying member of audience, useless person. Dead heat, result of race in which two or more competitors finish exactly level. Dead language."

Margaret abandoned the exercise, closed the dictionary and put it back where she had found it under the boys bed. Then she sat up and looked at herself in the dresser mirror. She had better freshen up a bit before going on Skype with her language student.

"Ohhh, what a dreary face you have my dear," her reflection critiqued.

"Speak for yourself."

"Tu chez...well?"

"What do you want?"

8

"Margaret, Margaret, my dear, surely you know."

"No, well, I suppose, there's so many things. The masturbation?"

"No, don't be silly and its not the copying from the dictionary either. "

"Ok, fill me in."

"Well, how long has Warren been gone, over four years, isn't it?"

"He's not gone. He's dead, dead, dead," Margaret yelled.

"Dead, yes, you' re right, love."

"What's with the Irish accent."

"I was going for Welsh."

"Ha, accents aren't your strength," Margaret said weakly.

"You can take the ring off anytime. You can be single again, it's allowed."

"Humph."

"How old are you, forty-eight. Just coming into you sexual prime."

"Forty- seven," she answered looking at the floor.

Margaret quit fussing with her ring and looked back at her reflection. She cleared the croak from her voice.

"Just coming into my sexual prime?"

The reflection smiled and nodded.

"Well, I'm certainly past my reproductive peak."

"You know what I mean professor."

"I'm not a professor, I'm a tutor."

"You know more than any long nosed professor at that university."

Margaret sat quietly for a moment, then shrugged and spoke, broodingly.

"I haven't got time for this right now."

"Oh, come on. Lighten up. It's nearly Valentine's Day."

Margaret walked into the hallway and picked up the laundry basket. The flurries were falling lightly at the moment. How quickly and quietly a thin layer of snow had accumulated on the cold ground. The country lane that passed by her old farm house was without a track. It had been a long winter. February was the cruelest month.

Margaret looked away from the window and toward the bedroom at the other end of the hallway. It's door was open and she could see her steamer trunk. The trunk had been sitting there, in that spot, for nearly thirty years. Above the trunk was a window. In the distance was the battle ship grey of the bay. It felt as if she had dragged the great green strong box up from that bay and now it waited just to cross the Atlantic again. But deep down Margaret knew, this rocky windswept shore was its final resting place, as would be hers.

She caught herself fussing with the ring again, then glanced at her wristwatch.

"Oh god, I better get moving."

Margaret took a quick step. She was closer to the stairs than she realized and her foot struck the second step with a thud. She fell four more steps to the landing, slamming the side of her head and forearm against the wall. The ulna broke near the wrist and dazed, she fell sideways the remaining ten steps down to the kitchen floor. Margaret lay still, wondering if she could move. The pain in her head was intense and her arm had a weird kind of numbness. Opening one eye, the light was so painful, she quickly closed it again. That felt better. She felt a great desire to go to sleep. Sleep seemed so inviting that her breathing and pulse responded accordingly.

"Hey, get up, wake up."

Margaret pulled up on one elbow. The wooden rocking chair at the foot of the stairs waddled its way toward her, speaking.

"You can't fall asleep. You might have a concussion. You can't sleep."

Then the stove agreed, "That's right, no sleeping, absolutely *forboden*."

Margaret put some weight on her broken arm and moaned. She managed to sit up carefully holding the broken arm

"That's it, get up, have a glass of whiskey," said the little cot by the kitchen window.

"What is this?" she asked.

"The society for the diffusion of useful knowledge," the table replied.

"Try to fix your arm. Just sit in my lap," said the rocker.

Margaret sat in the chair and began to rock. The rocker cot table, and stove began singing with gusto.

By yon bonny banks and by yon bonny braes

Where the sun shine bright on Loch Lomond

There me and my true love spent mony happy days

On the bonny, bonny banks o' Lock Lomond

Oh, I'll tak the high road and you'll tak the low road

And I'll be in Scotland before ye

But wae is my hert until we met again

On the bonny, bonny banks o' Lock Lomond

"Have a drink," said the table.

"On the rocks," said the cot.

Margaret sat in the rocker, a scarf wrapped around her wrist and with a glass of whiskey in her good hand made a toast. "Slange-ava."

Margaret watched the moving clouds through the kitchen window. They were moving swiftly northward. There was a brief break in the cloud cover and the south lying sunlight highlighted the snow-covered alder limbs outside the window. In the distance the shaft of light ran like a searchlight across the bay. Soon it was gone and the snow began to fall again. Margaret stood and turned on the radio. The Jews and the Palestinians were hard at it again. She turned the radio off and remembered her language student.

Margaret walked to the room that doubled as her office and fired up the computer. A thirty-something man appeared on the screen.

"I have an assignment," he said.

"An assignment?" she replied.

"Yes, are you familiar with kinbaku?"

"What about your German lesson?"

"This is, I need an educated woman's opinion. Could you help me with this assignment in kinbaku?"

"Kinbaku, what is it?"

"I'll send you a link."

In an instant the site appeared and Margaret opened it. There were a number of photos of kinbaku, a form of Japanese erotic bondage. Margaret perused the photos with a curious distance. 'These Korean lads', she thought, 'One odd group of puppies'. She returned to the student.

"Okay. What, ah, how can I... What's the purpose of this exercise?"

"The feminine held fast," he said.

"The feminine held fast?"

"Architecturally."

"Brilliant," she said, making no effort to hid the sarcasm.

"I've been practising with my roommate. He's quite feminine, I mean, he has a youthful girl-like physic. Here's a picture."

She viewed the photo of a long slender man tied up with dozens of one meter lengths of thin hemp rope. She compared the architecture student's efforts with those of the expert examples. To her novice eye it appeared the student had a reasonable understanding of the form. It seemed to Margaret that this was the strangest of strange sex play. She dallied with the images long enough to feel embarrassed by some sensations of arousal. It certainly was an activity reserved for those with too much free time.

"I my untrained opinion I would say, you have done well. Shall we get on with the German?"

"Yes."

They spoke in German.

"The can of soup is in the cupboard."

"What kind of soup is in the cupboard?" he replied.

"For Christ's sake, who cares about the soup in the cupboard?" the table lamp interjected.

"Do you mind?"

Margaret spoke sternly to the lamp, then looked back at the screen. The Korean architecture student was now a fish. The clock radio chirped in it's two cents worth.

"Fish can't do the kinbaku thing, they got no arms."

"Better than being in a permanent state of kinbaku, like you missy lamp," the fish replied.

Margaret felt the piercing pain in her arm. What was going on? Was she losing her mind? She couldn't let that happen again. It had been a couple years since her breakdown. Her mental breakdown.

"You fell down the stairs and struck your head. You struck your head," she said slowly.

Margaret focused on her breathing and looked at the fish on the screen. She laughed. It was the screen saver.

"God girl, you are a nutter."

She sent a message to her student. *The session today is cancelled. Sorry. Medical issue. I'll be in touch soon. Thank you.*

It was Monday, the day her son played hockey after school. He wouldn't be home until well after dark. Perhaps she could get her friend and neighbour, Helena, to drive her to the doctors, the emergency. Margaret picked up the phone. The line was dead. She looked out the window. It was snowing again and the wind had picked up. Sometimes the phone lines got damaged in bad weather. That must be the problem. Could she drive herself? That seemed like a bad idea. She could walk to Helena's? It wasn't that far, a kilometer, maybe less. She had done it many times.

Margaret began to panic as she dressed to go outside. She went to the pantry, poured a healthy ounce of whiskey into a shot glass, then tossed it back before leaving through the back door. The cold air and whiskey were competing sensations. The snow was only above her ankles, although it was accumulating quickly.

The pain in her arm was considerable now and she wondered if it was possible to set the bone herself. Margaret stopped and looked back at the house a couple hundred meters behind her. Near the house, her tracks were already filling in. The blowing flakes were larger now and were gathering on her clothes and eyelashes. She turned again toward the road at the crest of the hill. There were no tracks on the road either, but surely someone would drive buy soon. The snow wasn't that deep yet. She could flag someone down if she walked along it. Nearly everyone who used that road knew her.

Margaret adjusted her wool scarf over the lower half of her face and felt the warmth of her own breath. She could hear her own breathing and it surprised her how steady and calm it was. If Warren was still alive, he could easily set her arm. He was good at that kind of thing, a natural healer, good at first aid. A stick or pencil to span the break and then wrap it with her scarf. She could hear his voice telling her the best way to do it.

There was a long field behind the house that was lined by a windbreak of black spruce. She was close to it and the snow seldom penetrated through there dense limbs. It would be easy to find suitable splint making materials on the needle covered earth under those trees.

"I'm coming," she said as she trudged away from the road and across the drifting snow. Her stride was slow and laboured, but her will was steadfast, and upon reaching the sheltered grove she found two dry sticks the length of elbow to wrist. With her one hand she created the splint for her forearm. The pain was greatly reduced because of the support and she felt quite proud of her efforts.

Margaret sat on the dry needles and looked across the gentle slope of the field to her old farmhouse at its base. Faint smoke swirled in the wind above the chimney. She watched the scene for some time and as the wind eased the smoke went into a graceful curl and the snow flakes grew larger and fell straight down.

"Kind of looks like a Christmas card."

"Yes, its lovely, but I better go back now."

"Oh, there's no rush."

"No, you're right. This is perfect. I'm not cold at all," she said.

It was a long minute before Margaret looked in the direction of the voice.

"I can't see you, Warren."

"You will soon enough."

Margaret looked back at the farmhouse. Daylight was waning. The clouds began to clear. Soon the snowing stopped and slowly, silently, it was night. A light came on in one of the farmhouse windows.

"Grant is back. What about Grant?" she said.

"He'll ask for us when he needs us," he said.

Margaret looked in the direction of the voice. She could see Warren now, his silhouette. He sat on a stump, his youthful posture solid and erect. She recognized him right away.

"Is that how it works?" she said.

"Sure."

"He's a masturbation machine."

"All boys are," he laughed.

"Humm, he's a man now."

Margaret rested her face on her knees.

"Do you want to hear a tune?" Warren asked.

"A tune?"

"On the accordion," he said

She heard the bellows open and saw his nimble fingers play a flurry of cheerful notes, but didn't answer.

"How about 'The Irish Washerwomen?'" he answered for her and played.

Margaret couldn't help but smile when the joyful music filtered up through the snow covered spruce boughs into the star filled sky. Across the bay she joined the distant northern lights dancing.

Grant picked up the phone but the line was dead. He went back to the kitchen and again touched his mother's cold body where she lay, after falling down the stairs. He stood and looked at the laundry basket on the landing and his sheets on the steps. He had seen enough dead animals to know she had been dead for a few hours. It was cold in the kitchen and he opened the lid of the wood stove. Only a few red embers lay at the bottom of the fuel chamber. He lay in some fir kindling and placed a piece of hardwood on top of that. The kindling started to crackle before the stove lid was back in place.

Then he heard a familiar sound and he looked out the kitchen window down towards the bay. It was the snowplow slowly coming up the hill with its bright lights shining on him.

The Wind

The little bird was buffeted by the wind away from the flat roof and its shallow pond. His kin, a hundred and fifty odd of them, had just left the roof to a nearby perch of hydro wires and transformer cylinders. They felt the warmth of the power surging within the transformers and the bright light from the western sun. The little bird tumbled, corrected himself, and darted directly to a vacant spot on the uppermost wire. He chirped frantically.

"Holy Macaw. Did you see that? I, I, like I, rolled six times. Had to tuck my wings right up tight before I got my handsome beak into the wind. Wow."

His audience was already in flight before he finished and had caught his breath.

"Hey, wait for me."

He watched them head toward the harbour. He paced to his left, then right, felt a gust of air and rocketed off.

Down on the sidewalk, Yin Louie walked into the sun and wind. The wind kept his 88 year old methodical pace, super slow. He had dressed up a bit for the afternoon. Easter Sunday was as good an excuse as any to visit his old friend. Now heading home, his best blue raincoat and finely patterned pork pie hat shone brightly like the wet green grass. He steadied his progress with a black umbrella in his left hand. In his right he carried a white plastic bag of groceries which acted as a counterweight.

Yin steadied himself on the railing, down the stairs and entered the building. He unlocked his main floor apartment door. His thin wife was standing, looking through the glass patio doors. He spoke in Cantonese.

"What are you looking at?"

She turned and looked at her husband, but did not know who he was. He spoke again.

"So, what is it you see outside?"

She recognized his voice.

"The big white man was in the hallway," she said

Yin grunted and took off his coat.

"I saw him and came back inside," she continued.

Yin took off his hat and sat down. He sighed and asked.

"Which big white was in the hallway?"

"Which one?" She seemed surprised.

"Which big white man. The black hair, the red hair or the gray beard?"

"Gray beard, grey beard, him." She shuffled around the room and grasped the back of a stuffed chair

"Ah grey beard, grey beard, he likes you. He told me. He said, Mr. Louie, your wife is such a beautiful woman. You are a very fortunate man."

"He did?"

"Yes he has told me many times."

They were silent for a moment. Yin stood.

"Let's make something to eat."

His wife was looking out the patio door again. The small pine tree that hung over the fence rolled in the wind.

"Very windy," Yin said.

"I hate the wind," she replied.

"I know," he said quietly. Too softly for her to hear.

The block that Yin and his wife lived on was a short one. On the north side were three low-rise apartment buildings. Each building had about thirty suites. The south side of the street was less uniform. At the east end of the block was a box shaped three story place in need of repair. Most of the windows had sheets or blankets for curtains. It was rumoured the owner supplied drugs to the tenants inside. There was little doubt the folks on the inside were supplying drugs to a steady parade of visitors. Hard drugs.

The next building was another three story number with a couple of hip penthouses on top. It was well kept up with a new white and blue paint job. The manager spent a fair amount of effort pruning and preening the shrubs in front of the place. The next two buildings were the only houses on the block. The first was a purple arts and crafts cottage with a gay friendly rainbow flag. Two women shared the place, one big, one small, and they had two dogs, one big, one small. Parked in front of the place on the street was their old Mercedes sedan. Its long loud rattling diesel engine idle often woke gray beard in the mornings. "Jesus," he would curse, and peer out thru the Venetian blinds. The small woman in her animal control uniform would be fussing around the old beater. He mused he should show her his morning boner, but never did.

The next house was owned by a young couple with a toddler son and a newborn daughter. There was a basement suite with a young single mother. Sometimes she had a banjo playing house guest who would serenade the street from the front step. The big young black man loved to play slow hypnotic blues lines and tap out a plodding beat with a work booted foot on his banjo case. He was now a good ten minutes into one of these grooves.

Next to that was a weathered six suite apartment building. The property had only two tenants who lived on the middle floor. The two ground level suites and the two third floor suites were devoted to growing and curing pot. The middle-aged growers were old rockers going to seed. The woman still dyed her hair a rich blonde and always dressed in black. Her partner dressed only in black as well. His head was shaved and he sometimes wore a black choir gown on his errands about the neighbourhood.

Today the pot growing, dyed blonde, middle aged, gone to seed woman came out her gray door and walked out into the middle of the street. She flung bits of bread into the air, and shortly some crows descended to eat it. Then she marched in her long stride, her large backside jiggling within black spandex, back and forth across the lawn, watching the crows with great pleasure.

The banjo player ended his tune with little ceremony. The big foot stopped. He looked up to the gathering clouds and drew the collar of his jacket tight, then went into the basement suite.

Beside the grow op was a large vacant lot. The street ended here with a traffic barrier. Beyond the barrier was an industrial area which for many decades was the entrepreneurial grounds for street prostitutes. Other business included fish processing, a large poultry dressing factory, garment manufacturing, industrial style bakery, chandelier warehouse and an artist studio. The barrier was constructed by the city in an effort keep the bulk of the john traffic from cruising the residential area.

In the vacant lot, two Sikhs in turbans were erecting a high metal fence around the perimeter. A third man was picking up bits of refuse. The lot's owner was hoping to prevent a reprise of what had happened the previous summer, when the lot became a camping spot for drifters and homeless folk. It had also become a dumping ground for people's broken furniture. A man in a toque, eating an ice cream, came sauntering along the sidewalk. Coming toward him from across the barrier were two teenage hookers. They were marching in earnest to their drug dealers at the far end of the block. The three Sikhs looked up from their fencing to watch them pass. The tall one spoke in Punjabi.

"Surly a cold day to eat ice cream."

His fellow workers agreed. The sky had grown very dark, very quickly, and then suddenly the heavens burst with a great downfall of hail. It fell with vengeance, the small spheres bouncing off the green grass like popcorn in an oily pot.

The two girls stopped cold. The tall one hadn't slept for over thirty hours and she stooped precariously forward. She thought the earth was becoming covered with big rocks of crack cocaine. Her girlfriend tugged at her arm and pulled her back into their frantic pace.

"Mary, Mary. Come on, J.C. is waiting."

The migratory birds sheltered themselves from the hail in the dense boughs of the pine that overhung Yin's patio.

"What the heck is that stuff?" the yearlings chattered all at once.

"Hail," an older bird volunteered.

"Hail the hail," the smart aleck youth chirped. His baby bird friends jumped in.

"Hail the hail. Hail the hail. Hail the hail."

The older birds rolled their eyes and huddled a little closer together seeking greater warmth.

Back on the street a yellow cab stopped in front of the house of the young couple with the toddler boy and baby girl. The jet-lagged grandmother willed herself out of the cab, the wind lifted her strawberry hair up into a globe, just to plunk down again when she entered the gate. As her daughter with slightly darker strawberry blonde hair came down the stairs to greet her, the falling hail came to an abrupt stop. The son-in-law stood on the veranda holding the infant. Beside him danced the toddler.

"Grandma, grandma," he shouted. "Grandma, grandma."

Across the street, on the fourth floor, Patty sat in front of her computer reading an e-mail from her husband, who was travelling in Indonesia. Lincoln stood beside the bed buttoning his shirt. He walked over, put his hands on her shoulders and nuzzled her long, slender neck. She raised her hand and held his carefully.

"What's he have to say?" he asked.

"Oh nothing, nothing really."

In the alley a man was searching through the dumpster. A large bag of empty cans and bottles was balanced on the handle bars of his bicycle. The limbs of Yin Louie's pine tree arched overhead of the shiny purple dumpster with its gaping lids just inches below the clusters of long pine needles. The wind had eased and the trees branches barely moved. The sun had returned now, for a brief moment, soon it would descend below the horizon. Only the rooftops felt its warm glow.

Gray beard came shuffling down the pathway with a bag of garbage and a bag of empty beer cans. He startled the man in the dumpster, who in turn, startled the birds in the tree. The two men watched the flock fly up. Higher and higher the little birds went until they disappeared into a small patch of blue.

Gray beard spoke in his gravelly voice.

"Ya' want these cans, man."

"Oh yes sir, yes sir. Thank you very much. And happy Easter to you, sir."

A Very Large Spider

Darrell pushed the rickety wheelchair down the sidewalk. His mother looked at the care home grounds, the pale grey sky and the care home itself.

"What building is that?" she asked.

"Tide-View Ma."

"Oh, of course, that's where I live."

"That's right. Do you want the wheelchair seat belt done up?" he asked.

"No. I won't fall out."

They rolled along in silence for a brief while.

"Where are you taking me?" she said.

"Just around the perimeter of the building. Is that alright?"

"Oh of course, anywhere is fine."

"It's warm."

"Is it? We can stop if you're tired."

"Want to look at the basin?" he said.

"Okay."

They stopped where there was a gap in the low alders that grew on the east edge of the Tide-View grounds. Darrell sat on a smooth stone beside the wheelchair. It was the end of a long hot summer. Most of the wild plants showed their age. The asters were in full bloom but many the clover flowers were past their prime and the dandelions had all gone to seed. He picked one and blew the seeds away. Then he plucked the crown of a Queen Ann's lace and could smell the sap from the broken stem on his fingers. He handed the flower to his mother and a tiny pea green spider came up from the underside taking a position on top of the intricate pattern of white petals.

"Hey, there's a little spider," she said, smiling.

They both studied the little creature. It glowed as if light shone through it. Darrell watched his mother's face. She appeared delighted. After a short moment she looked at her son.

"I remember when you were a little boy, you were always wanting me to make up stories. Remember that?"

Darrell said nothing and she continued.

"Why don't you tell me a story for a change?"

Darrell looked out over the basin. The tide was very low. He ran his fingers through his thick auburn hair, closed his eyes and imagined the tide coming in. "Okay," he said and cleared his throat.

The dark spider stood motionless at the bottom of the bathtub. The gray, late morning light came in through the little north facing window. The spider was watching a tall woman named Simian put her proboscis close to the window. Her warm breath showed on its glass surface. The window was the best view from her apartment, the only view, really. Directly ahead was a park with a grove of mature Douglas fir trees. Their dark, dense green limbs formed the immediate horizon line.

She crooked her head, the side of her forehead touching the glass. This angle showed a much more distant vista. She saw an urban landscape of houses, four story apartment blocks, streets and trees on the rolling topography that gradually descended to the harbour and its big city skyline. The small bit of salt water she could see was its usual calm and absorbed the colour of the dark forested mountains on the far shore. The mountain peaks were hidden with rain laden somber clouds. She could see a black hulled freighter and some of the bridge that spanned the inlet. She thought there was something magical and majestic about the way the downtown looked from a distance.

The naked Simian turned, sat on the toilet and urinated. The seat was cold against her skinny legs and she shivered just before noticing the spider.

"How did you get in there?" she said.

Not surprising, the spider didn't answer.

Simian closed her eyes, then opened them again. She had a cold or the flu, or a hangover. Maybe it was a combination of all three. She hadn't considered her eating regime. She'd cut down on protein and she'd cut down carbohydrates and fat was forbidden. Sort of, cheese cake was allowed.

She washed her hands and looked at her young face. There was a small pimple on her nose and she rubbed it. It was more noticeable now.

"Ahhh."

She washed her handsome face. The floor squeaked and the towel smelt a bit funky. Simian noticed her aroused nipples in the mirror. She turned in profile and straighten her back. Her ribs were well defined and they reminded her of the spider's legs. He was still there. She considered turning on the shower and washing the intruder down the drain, but instead she opened the little window a couple of inches, thinking it might find its way out. It seemed like a considerable journey, scaling the tub, the tiles, around the shower curtain, across the wall to the window ledge and then out.

She shifted the curtain away from the wall. Did the spider move? She knelt on the floor and leaned closer. What long legs and so absolutely still. The young woman stood.

"Okay, Dandy, Daddy Long Legs, escape."

In the kitchen, she made some hot water and turned on her little computer. The sound of the fridge made her head hurt, so she unplugged it. With a cup of lemon echinacea herbal tea beside her, she typed in spider. A list popped up. Spiderman, spider solitaire, spiderman cartoon. Simian scrolled down the list and clicked on the Spiderman cartoon theme song. It was a clever one minute, two second song and graphic. She played it again, and then noticed 15,618,976 views of it had come before her. Simian remembered her father singing the tune while doing his silly dance when she was a child.

Looking at the screen made her feel ill and she turned off the addictive machine. Then she lay on the bed and wished her father was there to look after her. The thought gave her some comfort. After a minute, she got up, went to the bathroom and checked on the spider. Still there, hadn't moved. She took the funky towel and put it in the laundry basket, then prepared to go out. It was raining, but she wore good rain gear and the movement and the fresh air gave her a glimmer of vitality.

The spider picked up its front legs and rubbed them together. There was a sound although it is very difficult for people to hear. Spiders hear it and the spider amused himself with his fiddling. It sounded a bit like 'Turkey in the Straw'. After a few minutes of overture the arachnid went for a little stroll around the bottom of the tub, warming up for the difficult journey ahead.

Quickly, with powerful strides he scaled the tub, then up the wall and onto the ceiling. He stopped for a moment, upside down, with the blood flooding into his brain. Soon acclimatized to the new perspective, the spider oriented his self on a direct route toward the mirror. With careful, casual confidence he made his way across the ceiling. Above the mirror he anchored a thread and lowered himself down to the center of the mirror. He looked at himself, then did a few trapeze tricks before stopping again to reflect upon his reflection.

It was a long reflection and bittersweet. This was nice. He'd miss having eight legs, but this just wouldn't do. He closed his eyes and focused deeply. The transformation started with the front right leg. It took on the appearance of a right human arm. Then the front left leg became a left arm. The four hind legs merged in two human legs. The body and head also shifted into human form. The last two legs came together and formed a penis.

He studied himself in the mirror. His colour was still a beautiful black, but unlike his spider self, he was unusually well-endowed. He shrugged and smiled and instantly began to grow. Soon the weight broke the thread and the tiny man landed on the sink. He grew bigger and bigger until he could reach up and touch the ceiling. It was a happy sensation touching the ceiling again and he just stood there for a while. For some strange reason his hands just wouldn't stick to the ceiling surface. That was disappointing. Then he hopped off the sink onto the toilet. Luckily, Simian had left the seat down. He stepped to the floor and in front of the mirror. The little fellow had to stand on his toes to see the reflection of his whole face.

"Hello," he smiled.

The man who previously was a spider wandered about naked in Simian's apartment. He looked in the laundry and found the funky towel and smelly socks, which interested him. He checked out the fridge. There was a nearly empty jar of olives, two pieces of cheese cake and a small bag of baby carrots. The man wasn't sure why, but he felt obliged to plug in the fridge, which he did. Noisy old thing, he thought.

He explored the apartment for some time, looking in cupboards and closets. Feeling cold, he put on some of Simian's clothes. The underwear drawer was a cornucopia of styles and colours; red, pink, blue, white, yellow, and his favourite, gold satin. The small man shimmied on the elegant undies. He was particularly pleased with the way the shiny material accented his thick cock. It looked like a great golden dolphin diving into the mysterious depths. Simian's fantastic spider web pantyhose were too long but he kept them on and the puffy pale pink blouse fit perfectly. The last item that kind of fit was a green toque with little red reindeer. Finally he wrapped a blanket around himself and sat in a chair looking out the window. The rain was coming down heavily and the tree limbs thrashed vigorously from the gusting wind. The window rattled. "What now?" he thought.

*   *   *

For Simian, the violent sea was an old friend. It was what she did when she was a child. Ride her bike to the seaside and watch the storm roll in. She loved to stand face to face with the power of the nature, just meters away, defying it, mistress of the universe.

Today, Simian secured her bike on a metal post and walked a short distance along the seawall as the wind gathered greater and greater strength. As the waves crashed against the seawall and the spray hurled high above her, a jolt of ecstasy coursed through her. She raised her arms and yelled.

"Bring it on. Bring it on."

Her fascination with its vitality emboldened her beyond common sense. When she noticed the sea was damaging the stone foundation of the walkway, the young woman finally realized her safety was in danger. The wind suddenly blew more forcefully, she turned her back to the storm and clung to the rock face that bordered the walkway. Looking back toward the bike, she saw a hole forming in the seawall. The fine stone and mortar work tumbled into a pile of rubble two meters below to the rocky beach. Instinctively she moved hand over hand, long fingers grasping crevices and the sinewy plants that grew out of the cliff that rose above her. Fifty meters away was the bicycle, fastened to a handrail, where the walkway was built on solid earth. That was the closest spot where Simian could get off the seawall and find shelter in the forest. Small stones and clay were sliding down the rock face. Above, she could hear one hundred year old conifers snapping in half and then their thud as they struck the water soaked earth.

Thirty meters to go and she stood at the edge where the seawall had given way. A narrow section of asphalt still remained attached to the vertical cliff-face. Cautiously she stepped onto the thin ledge suspended over the angry sea. Three strides across and then Simian looked back. She watched as the asphalt fell, silently joining the granite building stone below, the sound drowned out by the raging fury. Twenty meters to go, the fierce wind clutched at her, trying to pull her away from the rough cliff. Ahead the bike clattered against the railing. Hand over hand over hand she inched along. With fifteen meters to go grasping the cold sharp rock face caused Simian's fingers to bleed. Ten meters to go and above her a great hemlock was struck by a falling cedar. The hemlock tumbled over the rock-face, its crashing crown pierced the stony beach below her, its roots hung from the cliff's pinnacle. The tree limbs, thick as her thighs, splintered all around her. The sound so intense she covered her ears. She was caged by dense and splintered limbs. It was dark and she held her breath. She dare not move.

Finally, she had to breathe and she turned her face from the stone. Another breath, and the smell of the tree instantly had a calming effect on her. Slowly, Simian's eyes grew accustomed to the limited light. She was alright. She laughed nervously, lowered to sit, wondered if she should stay put. Pulling herself into a tight ball she closed her eyes. It was cold but it wasn't that bad. The trees bulk absorbed much of the wind and wave. She would just rest for a few minutes.

*　　*　　*

The small man who had been a spider wondered when his host would return. He noticed a flyer from the food court at the Pacific Mall. He phoned the number and asked for Simian.

The person on the other end said she didn't know anyone by that name, but if she came by she could pass on a message. She also said that the mall might close early because of the storm. She apologized for that.

"Who should I say has called?" she asked.

The man who once was a spider paused a moment. He didn't have a name. His eyes wandered about the desk.

"Current," he said.

"Current. Is that your first or last name?"

"Ah, first. Current English," he read the book's title next to the phone.

"Current English?"

"Correct."

"Okay Mr. English, thank you, have a nice day, good bye," she said and hung up.

"Thank you."

Mr. English put down the phone and and turned on the computer. He saw the previous addresses Simian had visited.

"Ah, ha, she is an amorous arachnid, just like I suspected."

Gleefully, he watched some of the Spiderman cartoon, then abruptly turned it off and scowled. All that nonsense about spidy-sense irritated him. Current stood and paced. Where the hell was she anyway? Just like a broad to keep a guy waiting. He put his hands against the window and felt the vibration caused by the storm. He thought about why he was angry.

"Chill dude, it's not her fault, it's just a cartoon," he whispered.

Current decided to play a little tune and rubbed his arms together. Nothing. This was disappointing. He looked down at the poorly fitting, spider hosiery on his short muscular legs. He wondered if it was a kind of omen, a metaphor for not fitting in. He sat down and rubbed his cold feet together. Scuff, scuff, scuff.

"That ain't music either."

Current went into the bedroom and lay down on the bed. He aimlessly picked up the newspaper on the nightstand. There was a man on the front cover in a big blue suit with a mask on his face that sort of looked like a spider. He read the caption. 'Shut out Sam'. The guy was a hockey player, a goalie. There were a lot of of articles in the paper about the hockey players. More than anything else, he guessed. Simian likes hockey players who try to look like spiders. He smiled and closed his eyes. He pictured her as he had seen her in the bathroom. Those ribs, wow, just like spider legs. Oh man, he was getting a boner. What now?

The phone rang. Current sat up. Maybe it was her. He picked it up.

"Hello."

"Ah, hi, ah, this is Tom. Ah, is Simian there?"

"No, she not here."

"Oh, well, I'm her dad. She usually phones on Sunday afternoon. Who am I talking to?"

Current said honestly he had just dropped in and that he would relay her father's concerns. He sensed the father's anxiousness and then Tom said, "Well, maybe she just went out somewhere to watch the game."

"Shut out Sam, our great leader," Current replied.

Tom's voice got excited. He recited a mother-load of hockey lore: the names of the players, their jersey numbers, their age and what position they played. Perhaps this was a code, Current thought, and he quickly started to write numbers and names on a sheet of paper.

"Borrows, 14?"

"Exactly."

Tom continued talking: numbers of goals, assists, penalty minutes, ice time, goals for, goals against, salary caps, travel distances. Current was stumped. Being human was way more esoteric than he could have guessed. Then it dawned on him. It was their pantheon of gods. How quaint. Current laughed.

"What's so funny?" Tom asked.

"Oh, nothing. I just sneezed."

They spoke a little longer and then signed off. Current lay down again. He felt discouraged. Perhaps this transformation into a different species was a mistake. Maybe this feeling was melancholia, the feeling his spider clan had warned him about. These human creatures seemed so remarkably backward and superstitious.

He listened to the storm for a while. Night was beginning to fall, and the wind and rain seemed to be easing off a little. Then he reminded himself why he dropped in in the first place. Those ribs, holy-moly, Simian's righteous ribs. Current rolled on his side and closed his eyes. The owner of the bed would probably be home soon, 'just relax', he told himself. Beds were a fabulous invention for such a backward species. He smiled and fell into a peaceful sleep.

*   *   *

Simian surveyed her evergreen prison. Her eyes had adjusted to the dim light. It was remarkable that none of the great tree's limbs had struck her. She considered her fortune to be a good omen. A large wave came and lifted the crown of the tree slightly, and then it dropped down again. A stone fell from the roots at the top of the cliff and struck the trunk with a drum-like thunk. Simian struggled to stand and started to run on the spot while flailing her arms.

"My god, I'm freezing," she whispered.

Keep moving she thought and the tree lifted again causing more stones to fall. The tide must be rising and she got down and crawled, then slithered into the dense mass of limbs. She pushed and pulled at the wall of matted limbs and then her hand poked through. She started breaking the smallest new growth till there was a hole she could see through. There was her bike a half a body length away. The tall woman rolled on her back, bent her knees and placed her feet on a thick branch. From this power squat position she waited and listened. Waves were like contractions, they came in sequence, each one getting more powerful. The big one might lift the tree again.

Simian's timing was precise, the tree lifted, she pushed her upper torso through the gap, grabbed the front wheel of the bicycle and pulled her childbearing hips and long legs free before the tree settled down holding her feet fast. She immediately sat up, pulling at the limbs when a high wave pulled her over the edge of the seawall. She hung there upside down, held by her feet, suspended like Houdini, screaming into the roar of sea and wind. With her broad shoulders to the wind, Simian managed to get her body back on the walkway, hands again clinging tightly to the bicycle wheel. Wave after wave washed up on her as she fiercely held herself in place.

It remains a magician's secret as to how she managed to get her right foot out of a laced up boot, but at this she succeeded. The barefoot squirmed free and the left booted foot easily followed. Simian pulled her self onto the moss that borded the path. She gathered the bike's ruck sack and struggled up the steps and into the dark tangled mess of forest. The great trunks lay one over another over another. Many had their roots turned up, great pancake shapes of rock and root and soil meters high. This kind of storm didn't happen here, she reasoned. The world must be changing, the world was changing. She found shelter in a miniature cathedral of cedar boughs and Douglas fir limbs. There was nothing left standing to fall on her.

Night was coming on quickly and she was hopeful the wind was starting to wane. Leaving her little bivouac was tempting, but wisely Simian prepared to stay the night. She opened her rucksack. Inside the sack was a lighter and a candle, one can of ginger ale, one apple, a pair of gloves, and wool socks. Simian drank the ginger ale, fitted the burning candle into the can's opening and began pushing the loose top layer of soil, leaves and needles, into a ring around her. She would try to build a little nest, a kind of cocoon. Slowly the drier earth began to show, then she hit a flat wooden surface. She tapped the wood with her knuckles. It had a hollow sound.

Simian worked the ground away to reveal a rectangular wooden box that she lifted out of the ground. The box was less than a half meter in length, over a quarter meter in width and a little less than that in height. She curled up in a tight ball and stared at little coffin-shaped box. The candle flickered and went out. Simian felt around in the dark finding the lighter and relighting the candle. Simian pushed the little coffin to the far side of her nest Then she focused on her shoe less foot. The nursery rhyme went through her head.

Little diddy dum-dum my son John,
Went to bed with his stockings on.
One shoe off and one shoe on,
Little diddy dum-dum, my son John.

*　　*　　*

Current woke suddenly. In his freshly formed human mind an image glowed, a single boot held fast to the wet pavement by a web of green needles. The short man felt well rested. He hopped up and strode to the window. The whole city was dark, the power was off. His eyes adjusted well to the dim light and he looked through the kitchen until he found a working flashlight. "Ah, ha!" he said. Then Current rooted around the laundry basket. Cautiously, he sniffed a pair of socks while reflecting on the erotic notion of the human scent. Current shrugged. It was no doubt an acquired taste. Current English put on a pair of sneakers. "Same smell, wow, potent."

A leather bomber jacket hung from a hook on the entry door and he put it on. It was a little too big. "Gees, this is gonna be fun, find the woman who owns the smelly socks."

He walked for, what seemed, a very long time through the city without electricity, along quiet streets, around and over fallen hydro poles and broken trees. He moved quickly and within an hour he made it to the seawall. With the aid of a flashlight Current located the bicycle. He could smell the boot scented with hemlock and picked it up.

"Now, the babe," he said and walked up the steps into the tangled mess of fallen trees.

"Simmeeeonnn."

Soon he heard a voice and followed it, nimbly crossing the storm's destruction. She saw his flash light.

"Help, help, over here."

Current crawled into her timber cavern and sat up. They looked at each other in the dim candle light. He introduced himself and added. "Your dad was looking for you."

"He's here?"

"No, he phoned. He thought you might be watching the game."

She looked at him blankly.

"What's that?" he said pointing at the box. She said nothing. He opened it.

"Oh, Its a skeleton," Current said.

"I knew it. I knew it," she blurted.

He reached in the box.

"There's a note, 'Scruffy's gone. We're so sad. Best damn cat we ever had.'"

"A cat?"

Then she started to cry and laugh. He watched her, a little confused, then said, "I got your boot. It's kind of wet though. Do you want to hang out here or go home? Should we bring Scruffy with us?"

She was laughing more than crying now. What a strange fellow, she thought.

"Maybe best to bury it," she said.

Current English liked that idea and got right to it. This was the most spidery he had felt since he left the bathtub.

Simian sat on the cross bar as Current peddled the bike along the littered streets. She was happy.

"We're supposed to wear helmets in case we fall," she said.

"Oh, we won't fall. I have a great sense of balance."

It was true she thought, how gracefully the bicycle glided along, his long arms on each side of her, his warm breath on her neck. She was sure she could hear his heart beating remarkably fast as they climbed up the hill toward her street. Cherry blossoms were scattered everywhere in front of the big old house with her top floor apartment.

Inside, Current turned on the gas oven and opened the stove door. He closed his eyes and slowly rotated in the heat that poured out. The little man removed the wet clothes until he was only in the shiny gold underwear. What an odd fellow indeed, she thought, although she had to admit that those undies never looked better. His expression was the definition of innocence and given the circumstance, stripping down to one's underwear seemed like a decidedly sensible idea.

The heat felt wonderful as Simian did the slow motion Dervish twirl in tandem with the man who once was a spider. Current opened one eye and saw Simian's backside jiggle and then those tantalizing ribs. She peeked at him and noticed the underwear no longer contained him. Her hero's erection stuck out like a beautiful divining rod. Simian followed her intuition.

"Take a hot shower with me."

Her voice was music to his ears.

They stood together under the hot water and washed each other, taking turns applying the soap. She turned off the water and they patted each other dry. Current was delirious with desire and Simian was ready to receive. They finally kissed and something strange and miraculous happened. Her arms tuned into four long spindly legs as did each leg became a pair of spindly spider legs. Her body and head changed too. The same thing happened to Current and as they changed they became smaller and smaller until they were two spiders at the bottom of the tub. She was twice as big as him as that is their sexual dimorphic lot.

Everything for Current now seemed to be happening at once. He released sperm from his genital opening on the abdomen while shooting out web thread from the spinnerets on his rear end. With the webbing he wrapped the sperm in a neat little package. Current carried it with his padipalps, the two antenna-like appendages that is a part of his mouth. He mumbled an ode to her epigyne, Simian's pet name for her genital opening.

"Less talk, more action," she said.

She was a very large spider, a very large thin spider. They were the dangerous ones, the hungry ones. He must play his strongest card. It was a tried and true family tradition, the significant sacrifice play. Current ripped off his left front leg and offered it to her. Simian, a beast of fine breeding, daintily savoured the delectable gift. Her lover was already between her lovely legs and face first into her love chamber he delivered his precious cargo. Simian liked him so much she could just eat him up. Why not? She needed the protein.

Now, for Current time was of the essence and a hasty retreat was in order. He made a run for it, less nimble on seven legs. Getting up the side of the tub presented an obstacle he hadn't planned on. Sideways seemed to work.

"Current, don't run away."

"Spin a web, catch some flies, keep me out of it," he said.

She was making ground, enjoying the pursuit.

"I want you."

"I want to live."

They were both on the tiles now and he could see the ledge and its open window.

"Wait, Current, wait."

"It's not you, it's me."

In the living room the phone was ringing. Simian stopped and glanced in the direction of the sound. Who would call this time of day, and then she remembered. Her folks would be worried sick wondering how she was. She certainly had a story to tell. Well, at least some of it.

She looked back at the window. Nothing there but the faint glow of dawn. She shrugged and walked slowly to the ceiling and then even slower across it. Simian lowered on a thread, stopping in front of the mirror. The steam on the glass was quickly fading clear. Swinging in a short arc, she put her two legs together and began to make little fiddle sounds only spiders can hear. It was a song her mother used to sing,

The rinky dinky spider, went up the water spout,

Down came the rain and washed the spider out,

Out came the sun and dried up all the rain,

And the rinky, dinky spider went up the spout again.

Darrell's mother sat with her eyes closed.

"Mom, are you awake?"

"Yes, thank you dear. I'll like to lie down for a while."

"Okay."

Darrell wheeled his mother toward the entrance of the care facility.

"You know, after your father died, I dated a man, Jackson was his name. He was an American, had a summer place down Digby Neck. He lived there year round after he retired. He was a widower too. It didn't last long. I gave him up. He just wasn't the man your father was."

"Ah, uh."

"I liked the story, by the way. Is it starting to rain?"

"Yes."

"God knows we need it. Its been a very dry summer this year."

"I'm heading back to Vancouver tomorrow. I'll drop in before I leave. Okay? "

"Drop in, yes, please do."

Horses Running on Frozen Ground

Ira opened one eye. He had an erection. Some things never change. He rolled onto his side, hoping to fall back into that sweet sleep world. Sadly, the sound of the fridge commanded his attention. Ira opened both eyes to see the glossy beige wall just a dozen centimetres away. He rolled over on his back and looked toward the window. The lower half was covered with a dark green curtain, but the upper half revealed pale grey clouds. He tried to picture the person from his dream who said, "Your mission is to get high."

The memory of a woman, an old woman came to him. He pictured her now against the grey sky, in tight black jeans, walking away from him. It was more of a sashay than a walk, a cultivated gait designed to make an indelible impression. He could see her turn and look at him. Her face made an equally strong impression. She was pale and gaunt beneath thin blond hair. The face reminded Ira of a Mexican death mask. The combination of desire and death was unsettling.

He sat up and looked around for his clothes lying on the floor. He put on his pants and shoes. Ira limped down the corridor to the communal lavatory. While he urinated he saw through the window a crow with a chunk of bread hopping around on a neighbouring roof. A seagull was stalking the agile crow.

"The race is to the swift," he chuckled.

Much relieved, Ira slid open the bathroom window and looked down at the sidewalk seating outside the ground floor cafe. It must have been around eight in the morning, because Philip and Earl were in their regular spots. Ira considered going down to join the two creatures of habit. No doubt they were talking about antiques, cars or motorcycles, topics that often made Ira's eyes glaze over. Another favourite was leaky roofs and congested buses. Of course there was the tried and true latest cancer diagnosis, and obligatory mastery of medical terminology, though Ira was as guilty as the next man with that bullshit.

"Not today," he said and plodded back to his suite. He lay on his bed in the opposite direction to how he had slept, looking back into the room. He reached over and pushed the curtain open allowing the light to flow in over his right shoulder. There was a small table in front of the window with a couple of books and a half cup of cold tea. He drank the tea and picked up a book titled *Betting Thoroughbreds*. He opened it at random. There was an example of a racing form dated July 29, 1974. Ira read down the list of the horse names: My Compliments, Our Dancing Girl, Some Swinger, Secret's Out, Precious Elaine (formerly named Idontlikehim).

"I don't like him, Christ," He closed the book and pictured the horses running, could hear the sound of the announcer calling the race. Eyes closed, smiling, he slid back into a half sleep. Ten minutes later he got up. There were a couple shirts soaking in the sink. Ira wrung them dry and hung each on a piece of twine that ran the width of the room, near the ceiling. The building had been a rooming house for a long time. One hundred and one years the landlord said. Ira figured drying one's clothes on a string over the stove had a long and venerable history. The ghosts were bound to approve. They should feel right at home.

Ira cleaned up around the kitchen counter. The clock said 8:59. The day was well under way and he felt like he had cement in his shoes. What day was it anyway? Friday, or Saturday? They say that's what happens when you work nights. You get the days mixed up.

"Friday night is date night," he said with animated conviction, addressing an open cupboard. "Precious Elaine," he added, and shut the cupboard door. How weird was that? Well, he had once known an Elaine. Hell, he had the tattoo.

Ira put a tablet of Vitamin B12 under his tongue. It had a sweet taste as it dissolved. A little bit of a woman's love and affection was way overdue. Ira's memory was a powerful instrument and it held sway in the present. Old flames were milling around his room, each one a class act. Someone had told him once that his greatest talent was meeting remarkable women. Ira mused it was a talent in hibernation. He took a half dozen vitamin D tablets.

Water with the pills? What a good idea. Ira shook his head. He was too hungover. Instead he ate a ripe pear and got ready to greet the outside world.

He buttoned his jacket, ran a brush through his thick hair, then glanced briefly at a small round mirror above his sink.

Something was very strange. Ira moved closer for a longer look. His watery blue eyes were such a dark brown they could be mistaken for black. His sandy brown hair was even blacker in the natural gray daylight from the window. His ruddy, weathered skin appeared bronze coloured and smooth.

Ira held the vitamin B container in his thick hand and tried to pronounce the ingredients.

"Methylcobalamin, mannitol, cellulose, xylitol, crospovidone, diacalicum phosphate, dextrose, vegetable stearic acid, vegetable magnesium stearate, calcium carbonate, silica."

He was only mildly unsettled that he had virtually no clue to what he had dissolved under his tongue. Better living through chemistry, he recalled. Silica. Wasn't that like sand?

Ira stroked his beard. He took a second look in the mirror, but saw a slender hand touching the taut skin of a graceful jawline. The eyes peering back at him were deep set and not his own. The nose was small where his was large. Ira turned his back on the reflection, mildly alarmed. Outside his window the birds were gone. He noticed patches of ice on the flat rooftop where he had seen puddles earlier.

"Humph. The mission is to get high?"

His thoughts drifted out of control. He began to muse on the odds associated with track conditions. Horses running on frozen ground. In his chest he could feel hooves striking the ground. The sensation made him dizzy. He walked slowly into the studio, where he began picking up the empty beer cans, putting them in a plastic bag. A guitar was leaning against a wooden chair in the centre of the room.

"Miss Harmony," he said, stroking the wood of his favourite instrument as he put her out of harm's way. He opened the curtain on the studio window. From here Ira could see the alley and the downtown core of the city, everything a darker gray than the sky. In the alley a woman was rooting through a dumpster for treasure.

At Ira's feet lay a pair of woman's boots. He picked them up and sat in the corner chair, holding the surprise find in his lap. He was at a loss to explain the presence of the soft deerskin footwear. He felt a little nauseous.

The room had a large full length mirror hanging on the wall, opposite the window. From his overstuffed chair he could see the reflection of the downtown skyline. The city scape in reverse usually amused him. It gave the illusion of being somewhere else. He looked at the boots, then back at the reflected city. He stood, swallowed hard, and stepped in front of the mirror.

In dismay Ira examined what was supposed to be his reflection. He saw a tall, young woman. She was wearing an open jean jacket and a small dress with horizontal bands of pale purple and hot pink, cut away at mid-thigh. She was the owner of the face he had seen in the mirror over the sink. Her long, skinny legs looked a little funny. She shifted her bare feet, put her hands on her hips.

"You like what you're lookin' at?" she said.

Ira almost nodded. "Who are you?" he said.

The young woman laughed. "You got a cigarette?"

"I don't smoke," said Ira.

"Just my luck. Got any dope?"

"I got weed."

"Anything else?"

"Anything else?"

"Coke, crystal, you know."

"Jesus," he scratched his beard and saw the reflection slide her fingers along her jawline to the cleft of her chin.

"I'll get you some money and you get me some dope," she said.

"Me?"

"The guy down the hall, Steve, he's got coke, speed, whatever."

"In number four?"

"Yes, handsome. Guy named Steve."

"Why don't you go see Steve yourself?"

The reflection laughed, darkly. She spoke in an old woman's tired voice.

"Steve, ain't nice to ladies, especially ladies that owe him money. You understand, don't you Ira?"

"Sure," he said unconvincingly.

She smiled and he liked the way she looked.

"What's your name?" he asked.

"Elaine, I'm Elaine."

"Humph, Well. What day is it?"

"It's Sunday, Ira, Every day is Sunday. Okay? We need some cash, honey, pronto."

Ira slid his bare feet into the boots. He didn't bother to look back at the mirror. He could imagine the presentation. Flat chested and willowy desperation masked by sexy determination. The woman walked down the hall, down the stairs. At the entrance she fussed a little with her hair, putting it together in a high ponytail. Elaine stepped outside and walked briskly down the alley, heading west the two blocks to her stroll. A car stopped.

"What da'ya do?" the guy asked though the half-open window.

"I can give you go, blow, half and half, hand act with trash talk."

"How much?"

The first three she quoted high. The fourth, which was easiest for her, she quoted low. It was a tried and true business strategy. So was the performance. Fuck the johns with their own sex babel. She talked dirty like a child as she jerked the guy's ugly noodle for sport.

Elaine made her kitty and arrived back at the apartment building with the heebie-jeebies closing in. She had difficulty getting the key in the door.

"Come on, come on. Stupid. Christ."

Inside she sprinted up the wide, worn stairs to Ira's suite. She looked in the full length mirror. She saw Ira.

"Money's on the bed, I need to wash. Go see Steve."

"There's coffee," he said.

"Go see Steve. Now."

When he came back, Elaine was no longer in the mirror. She was sitting on his bed. He gave her the goods and watched her get high.

"You?" she asked.

"No. I don't."

She laughed, and he thought her smile would melt butter.

"Do you have a girlfriend?" she asked.

"No, not really."

"Ha, well, not really! So what's that like? She's just in your mind? Hey, you sure like it warm in here. I may be a ghost, but I like warm. I think you need a girlfriend, Ira. Maybe I could be your girlfriend? I think you'd make a swell boyfriend."

Elaine kept shifting as she spoke, and Ira couldn't figure out where the sound was coming from. Her feet, no, her fingers, her eyes, her shoulder, the belly, her breasts, her face, her knees, her?

"I've been working the streets here since 1963, Ira. God damn. How long is that? Fifty years? Golden anniversary, right?"

"Golden?"

Elaine opened her housecoat to reveal a thin naked body.

"You like this?" she asked.

Ira nodded.

"Hasn't been a dick in there in fifty years! Fifty years of whoring and no man's cock has found itself into my pretty little pussy. I think I'm overdue sweetheart. I'm overdue for you."

"But you don't actually exist, Elaine. Do you?"

"Your mission is to get high, Ira. You're all mixed up."

Ira could smell fresh coffee brewing on the stove.

"You're a funny bunny, Ira. Come here,"

He took a step toward her. "You're not real, Elaine."

"I *am* real. I'm real, come here, come here."

She held out long thin arms.

He stepped closer. She undid his belt and his pants fell to the floor. He took off his shirt. She made him hard. As he mounted her, he saw her staring at the tattoo on his right bicep. It was a red heart with the name Elaine inside. He thrust himself into her. Deep in his chest he felt horse's hooves pounding on frozen ground.

The days are short in November. It was already dark when Ira fell asleep. Elaine listened to his breathing. She sat up and watched him. She was coming down, slowly, slowly for a change. It made sense. Elaine picked up Ira's pants and put them on. She went into the studio and stood in front of the mirror. All she could see were pants cinched around an invisible body.

"Didn't work," she whispered. She had been hoping to find herself in his skin.

She plopped down in the overstuffed chair. Ira's wallet was in his hip pocket and she pulled it out. It held a ten dollar bill. She put the rest of her own money in the wallet and slid it back into the pocket. She had enough dope to last the night, though she wasn't sure it mattered. She fell asleep for a while, and woke to the morning's first light.

Elaine found her clothes and put them on, leaving Ira's pants on the floor. She looked around what had been her small, precious home. It was the right time to leave. She opened the window and stepped onto the sill. A seagull standing sentinel turned its head to look at her. Elaine jumped. Up she rose just as the bird took flight.

In the bed Ira opened one eye. The morning rumble of the city penetrated his sleep-fogged brain. The air was cool and fresh. He noticed the window was open and stretched to close it, then buried his face in the pillow. After a few seconds he sat up.

"Elaine," he whispered.

He got up and went into the studio. In the mirror Ira saw his naked reflection. He was alone. He pulled on his pants and went down the corridor to the bathroom. Walking back to his suite he met the caretaker in the hallway.

"Hey Ira, Steve's leaving," said Carlos.

Ira looked confused.

"Steve, you know, in number four. He's a damn dope dealer, been wanting to get rid of him for a long time. We want good guys in here, like you brother."

"Yeah, umm, thanks Carlos."

The big man descended the stairs. Ira watched him go before returning to his suite. He warmed up cold coffee from the stove and poured it in his to-go mug. Outside Philip and Earl greeted him.

"Gees, haven't seen you in a while, my friend. Where you been?" asked Earl.

"Just catching up on my beauty rest."

"Can't say that it's workin' all that good," said Earl

"To sleep, perchance to dream?" added Philip.

"Dream? Yeah, I guess so," Ira sipped the hot coffee and continued. "So Phil, what's on your agenda this fine morning?"

"Oh, find a leak in my neighbour's roof and try to fix it."

"Lotta leaky roofs over his way," chuckled Earl.

"Owner's recently been diagnosed with cancer."

The rising sun was clearing the building on the east side of the street and warm light came slowly creeping down the cafe wall.

"How about you, Earl? Going for a ride?"

"Oh yeah. Take the motorbike for a spin, sure. Not many nice days like this left before the rains."

"What day is it, anyway?" asked Ira.

"Sunday man, Sunday all day."

"Ah, horses are running this afternoon."

Philip's long fingers plucked a long dark hair off Ira's jacket.

"Ha!" he said waving the evidence.

"Say Ira, who's the dark haired lady?"

Ira took the strand of hair and lay it on the chipped yellow paint of their little table. He was quiet. The others waited. People came and went from the busy cafe, carrying muffins and coffee, sandwiches and cakes. Cars and trucks stopped, then drove off. Families with baby buggies, folk with bikes, people with dogs. All coming and going, coming and going.

The Age of Misandry

"Now class, today we are going to cover the social history of the early twenty-first century, sometimes know as the Age of Misandry. I believe the term, like many esteemed historians say, is incorrect. But, because it is becoming more and more common in secular discourse we will spend a couple of lectures on this aspect of our historical overview of our Wenega Epoch. Now firstly, do any of you know what misandry means?"

The class of grade nines shuffled in their seats. None ventured an answer. Their electronic devices were always disabled during lectures.

One of the girls cautiously raised her hand. The other girls looked intently at her. "Pageantry using horses?" she said.

"Good guess but no. Anyone else?" Teacher said. After the silent moment she turned on the wall screen at the front of the classroom. "Okay, she said, "Let's read this together. Misandry was known to be the dislike of, contempt for, or prejudice against men and boys. Does everyone know what men and boys are?"

"Phalli," Monica said.

"That's right; an old fashioned word for phalli from pre-Wenega times," Teacher replied. The wall screen began showing a film of a man and a boy undressing and dressing. Many of the girls had seen the film before, but those from the orthodox schools had not. There the film was generally prohibited for girls under fourteen.

"You may have heard it was the phalli fault that we bleed. That's an old goddess myth created by overzealous wombs, nothing more. An old wives tale, to use another archaic term. Okay, enough of this," she said, turning off the wall screen and then playfully spinning like the phalli in the film. The girls smiled.

"Now. I know this an important year for all of you. This year is important for two things. Does anyone want to remind the class what those two things are? Yes, Fran?"

"If we complete our course work we get our own pleasure bots," she said excitedly.

"That's right. All girls must study hard and what else? Norica?"

"Have a good foundation for future success in whatever field we have an aptitude for."

"Correct."

"I want to be a judge," piped in Lorin.

"Me too," a couple of the other girls chimed.

"Ho, ho, yes, I know," Teacher smiled. "Oh to be a judge. Yes, it is the highest honour. But only one in twenty can become judges. Just one judge per class."

"I want to be a mother," another girl added.

"Yes I believe you Monica. I know you are a skilled athlete. How many babies would you like to have?"

"Five, the maximum."

"Oh, good, good. Do you have a fertile bot in mind or would you like a harem?" asked Teacher.

"I'd like a fertile bot like my mother has, a Billy Buck model."

The class all went "Ohhh" in unison and Mona visibility blushed.

"A Billy Buck model?" Teacher said, slightly blushing herself.

Then Miranda pronounced. "I want to be an accountant. I definitely want a harem."

"What kind of bot do you have, Teacher?" said Mona. "Oh, sorry."

"Well, I suppose it's okay to tell you, you're nearly fifteen after all. I was given a Grant. I was hoping for an Adam, but in my year there was an unusual number of high IQ's. So, I got a Grant."

"Is it a Grant, plus-plus?" a voice called from the back.

"The cuckold version or the threesome one?" another voice sounded.

"How do all you girls know all this stuff?" said teacher.

"Well we have bots as our mother's insemination servants and offspring guides," Monica replied with mocked innocence.

"Yes, we can thank the goddess Wenega for the virtue of uniformity," orated Teacher and the students' frivolity ceased. Teacher took a deep breath and changed the wall screen image. It was another archaic archival portrait of a dark skinned womb with a surprisingly serene presence.

"This womb is a controversial historian who wrote extensively on this period. We know her only as Octavia E, and at one time goddess Octavia, but in contemporary scholarship she is referred to as the false goddess. She does look goddess-like. Oh well. She lived during the transition from the archaic to the Wenega. Most of her works are long lost except for the long poem, titled by the phalli as 'The Age of Misandry'. What the original title was we don't know. In the poem she describes much of what we know from the early period. In it she tells about the rapid decline of phallic vitality, especially the sudden drop in sperm count, and a social tendency toward phallic self-emasculation. It's a mystery what the mechanics of these events were completely, but it is clear that the phalli were primarily obsessed with personal longevity and monopolizing the newest styles of pleasure bot. By today's standards the bots were terribly unsophisticated. Here's a line from the poem:

They thought with their little heads instead of their big
And with their bots, they did the jiggly jig jig."

A ripple of giggles went through the students.

"Yes, it's amusing to our more refined ears, but in her time the relentless unrestrained violations of the moral code had dire consequences for the wombs."

Moral code was an oft heard touchstone. Teacher's students sat erect, their gaiety compressed by a righteous atmosphere of solemn solidarity.

"We are wombs, all of us. Equal and strong," she continued.

"Equal and strong, equal and strong," they droned.

Teacher glanced back at the screen with Octavia E's picture. A fleeting second of doubt was attributed to an inadequate morning meal. Where was she? Ah, Tel-star.

"There was music," she announced and turned to the class. "Music, you may have heard it, Tel-star, found with the poem. It's been interpreted by experts to be an anthem commemorating the exodus of the phalli, the liberation of the wombs and with that the rebirth of the great Wenega."

Teacher played the recording.

"Beautiful isn't it? Ta, ta, taa, ta, ta, ta, ta, ta, taaa. Wonderful. Most of you had heard that before, yes?"

"Yes Teacher, we play it in band," Amy said.

"Oh, I see, very good. Okay, before I show this next image, I feel it's important to say that this photograph is from a time when pleasure bots were exclusive to phalli," and Teacher brought the image onto the screen. There was a wave of gasps and laughter.

"Yes, yes, the size of those breasts. It's hard to comprehend if these are the tastes of the builders or users. Since Octavia E leaves no evidence of earth-mother worship, to use an archaic term that might be used at the time, it's believed that these are simply primitive fetish objects rather than being true pleasure bots. Some claim it may have been a unfulfilled unconscious desire for womb worship. "

Teacher allowed the wall screen to fade to a pale pink glow and began to walk through the rows of students as she spoke. "As I said, it's difficult to determine precisely why the phallic sperm production declined so rapidly. Psychologically, environmentally, possibly both. Some historians claim that the phalli were lying to themselves. That's in a very liberal reading to Octavia E's poem. But, and this is important: Only phalli lie, wombs tell the truth."

She paced the parameter of the class and returned to face her students. "Wombs don't lie," she said in her call and response voice. In unison they responded. "Wombs don't lie."

"Good."

Teacher pointed at the wall screen and then #fuckthepatriarchy appeared. The blue coloured text seemed as if it was floating on the pale pink background.

"There were many siren calls against the phalli. This one has an obvious visceral rage. It's a derivative of the oft quoted, "Death to the patriarchy." Others were, "crush, destroy, kill, burn, drown the patriarchy, and so on. This was very much in the popular lexicon and within intellectual thought a rich tapestry of speech was constructed to support the concept. It was beautiful and righteous and of such massive volume that the pure weight of it metaphorically flattened the fertility of the phallic seed."

Teacher felt a little faint and realized she was becoming sexually aroused. She blew out a slow calming breath and turned toward the wall screen. An image of an infant, a few days old appeared.

"Okay. Wombs did a lot of research in artificial fertility. Obviously, the fact that we are here is testament to a significant degree of success. Although longevity is still problematic, experts are doing their best to improve it. Now, this little cutie known as K.D., often called Pauly, was the first child born with the genetically modified offy chromosome. Offy eliminates the development of the phallic gendered zygotes. It was a magnificent advancement in matriarchal empowerment. It freed us from having and to raise and care for phalli. Unfortunately, the offy chromosome went dormant after one generation. This decade was best memorialized by the popular hymn, 'Leave it outside the dome.'"

Teacher sang a couple bars, then checked the time.

"I'm getting a little ahead of myself here, besides you should be covering this material more in depth in your applied biology classes."

"Teacher?"said the tall girl in the back row. "I've been told that not all phalli became infertile, that there were a few outliers that became the foundation of our bot's genetic output. That these phalli were considered urberphallic and in fact, one of the best known was Summit Camps."

"Well, there's truth to the fact that during the earlier transition phases phallic sperm was used and code copied for fertile bots but that was soon synthesized from protein maps, a complete womb innovation. I mean, most genetic disorders are virtually unheard of. As for Summit Camps, the myth of his existence is, well, mythology," said Teacher, smiling.

"My mother, your equal, says the fact that I have one blue eye and one green eye proves I'm a descendant of Summit Camps."

"Your mother?"

"Yes."

"Where do you live?"

"In this dome?"

"Of course," said Teacher, with eyebrows raising.

"M parish."

Teacher wanted to ask what pleasure bot her mother had been assigned but she bit her tongue.

"You just had a tonsillectomy?"

The tall girl coughed out yes.

"You're feeling better?

"Oh yes, much better, thank you."

The end of class buzzer rang, the students left in silence. Teacher turned to the screen. She inadvertently returned the screen to the previous image, the cool blue #fuckthepatriachy floating in the warm pink eternity.

"Her mother, my equal. What nonsense."

*   *   *

The bus was noisy with chatter. Ear buds and headphones were forbidden. Teacher liked the emotions within the unknown languages. Sometimes she tried to guess what those people were saying. Through the din, she heard the sound of her mother tongue. It was an archaic word, grandfather. She looked for the speaker, but their identity remained a secret.

She walked to the apartment door past her neighbour's cat.

"Hello Teacher," the cat said.

Teacher wasn't required to respond and so she didn't. Inside she opened a plastic container. Leftover minced dog tongue that she gave the aroma test.

"Umm, heavenly."

She placed the container, a tomato and frozen algae on the counter, went into the studio, looked through some music, and clicked on Ellengar. Standing in front of a large mirror, she began stretching.

"Grant, make my dinner," she called out. Her bot disconnected from its charging station.

"Who've you been whoring with today?" Grant said.

"Oh, you know I wouldn't be doing something like that. Now be a dear, dear and get cooking."

He went to the kitchen as she danced. After a few minutes he said, "You've been listening to Elgar a lot lately."

"Ellengar," she replied and then stopped dancing and joined him at the stove. She studied the side of his head, thinking that she might see a bit of light through the cracks. Nothing. "Who have you been hanging out with? You feel alright? Talking to tel-star?"

"Um, no."

She didn't believe him. Grants were bad liars. It made a convoluted kind of sense but occasionally she felt a little mismatched. Grant seemed a bit down, why not cheer him up.

"I saw the janitor today. We were in his broom closet during a break."

"Oh, him, the old timer."

"Seventy isn't that old if you look after yourself. Duke's are known for their all round longevity."

"A cross section of Duke. Thank you bitch."

Teacher laughed, went back into the studio and sat in an easy chair.

"Would you like a glass of wine before dinner?" called Grant from the kitchen.

"Yes."

*   *   *

Tall Girl got off the elevated train at K station where it went underground and came out again nearly a kilometre ahead at L station. The round hill between the two stations was the highest in the dome and at the very top was a park from which you could see the vastness of the dome in all directions. There was a slender metal tower at the zenith with a sound-cancelling system that silenced an area around it in a radius of 275 meters. It was a wonderful sensation to hear the sounds of the city diminish as she walked toward the tower.

She sat on a wooden bench and noticed there was no breeze coming up the slope. Perhaps the wind machine was getting repairs. She started thinking about her conversation with Teacher in history class, again. She shouldn't have mentioned Summit Camps. And Teacher had asked her about her tonsils. She was surprised Teacher knew about it. Tall Girl turned on her device and typed in t-o-n-s-i-l-l-i-t-i-s and read the definition, ' A rare genetic disorder once common in the Pre-Liberation Period. Treatment often includes removal of tonsils. Non-fertility bot recommended as public health precaution'.

Tall Girl turned off the device and started down the hill toward the border of K and L Parish. The wind had started and soon she could smell the Norse slaughterhouse where her mother worked. She continued down past where the train emerged from the hillside and walked underneath the elevated tracks. Here there was an algae-alkaloid shop and an all day breakfast place that catered to the industrial workers in the western end of K parish. She would meet her mother here and then walk home together.

The a-loid brew shop was called The Sip. The owner Sue Sup spent much of her time in the bookstore at the back of the shop.

"Tall Gal," Sue Sup said.

"Hi Sue."

"Here to met your mom? You're early."

"Un,un."

"Everything okay? What's new?

"We're studying the age of misandry at school."

"Oh, hum, I wonder how they are gonna spin that one? You took the train today?"

"Part way, I went to the hill."

"Nice. You want an a-loid?"

Tall Girl nodded and sat on a stool at the south facing window. The great dome was still transparent and the light streamed in unfiltered. It was an accurate rendering of an archaic fall day. October 4th. The light entered the Sip window and fell on her hands, spread on the counter. Outside beyond the yellowing leaves of the alder tree were the elevated tracks. As the train passed, it cast a brief flickering shadow on her hands. She wondered if you could go faster than the speed of light would you really go back in time? They were taught that was what the phalli did. Climbed into their giant spaceships after mastering longevity and blasted off. To go back in time. Leaving the wombs to stay and heal the earth.

Sue sat the drink between Tall Girl's hands. "Mildly psychoactive inbound."

"Sue, do you believe that the phalli went back in time?"

"Well, they're not here, that's for sure."

"Mom says that..."

"Tall Gal don't go repeating what your mother says, okay."

"Yeah, I know. I'm afraid I did today."

"What did you say?"

"I was a descendant of Summit Camps."

Sue laughed. "We've all said that sometime or another. Still, your mother will go on about things." She looked around the shop and leaned closer, speaking softly. "You just have another year before you learn something practical and get your bot. You want to make baby wombs too, I bet."

"No, I don't think I'll be allowed. The tonsillectomy thing."

"Oh, I didn't know that. When was that?"

"Just last month."

"Oh, I thought you were at you sister's. You mother said...."

"Said what?"

"I must have misunderstood. Well, how do you feel about that?"

"I just might be expected to stay home and take care of Mom."

"Well, she's not that old," Sue Sup smiled.

"Fifty-seven."

"Fifty-seven. Wow, that's old. She doesn't look it."

"I bet she lives to 61 or 2, even."

"That's rare. Amazing, I would never have guessed. My mom was fifty-three when she died and that was considered average."

They stayed silent. Another train's shadow flickered past. Tall Girl sipped her a-loid.

"Any interesting new books, Sue?" Tall Girl broke their introspection.

"Some, but I'm mostly dealing in second-hand books these days. Oh, talking about the age of misandry, I just got a copy of a book written by a phallic. Come to the back, I'll show you."

In the back, off to the side of the bookstore was a little room where Sue Sup slept. From under the cot she pulled out a dusty, non functioning bot.

"A dead bot?" said Tall Girl.

"Yep, You know the nursery rhyme. 'If you don't like what mean bot said, make mean bot sleep under your bed.'" Sue playfully crossed her lips with one short finger. "Shusss. Fools the censors every time." Then she reached in farther and pulled out a cardboard box half full of books.

"I'm not selling these," she said. "Here it is. It's by Amenos. I looked that up. It's Greek for the wind."

Tall Girl held the book and read the title. "Bachelor Cooking and the Art of Seduction. What's seduction?"

"I think it must be an archaic animal mating performance, where the phallic tries to convince the womb to have sex with him."

"Why would they want to do that? Why not wait till the womb wants to have sex?"

"Phalli thought with their little heads instead of their big ones."

"Oh, okay, so that's what that means." Tall Girl said and opened the book. "Macaroni, cheese and a couple cans of sardines. Hum, that's an interesting display."

"Look, a burning candle shaped like an erect penis. I'm a little bit aroused, how about you?"

"Well? He has a nice red beard. There's a pleasure bot that has a beard isn't there?"

"A Carl, I had a Carl. I wore him out."

"You didn't get a replacement?"

"No. I think, I found books more interesting. Ah, there's somebody in the front, maybe it's your mom. Take the book if like, but, well, best keep it a secret, just in case, you never know who might disapprove."

"Okay," Tall Girl said and dropped the secret into her shoulder bag.

The mother and child stood in front of the cooling cup of a-loid, as Sue busied herself with the few abandoned customers. Mother took a drink from the cup as Tall Girl sat.

"Don't mind, do you?" she said and Tall Girl gave a shrug. Her mother continued, "Umm, good. How was school?"

"Fine."

Mother sat on the stool beside her. "Nice day isn't it."

Tall Girl began to reveal her day at school and mother appeared the good listener all the while her mind running through a familiar script of her daughter. She was the youngest of five wombs, four of whom had been born before she was thirty. Tall came as a surprise eleven years later. From her earliest days Tall Girl was different. Her wild weed.

"Teacher seemed a bit irritated by it all," Tall finished.

"Good, she needs to be challenged."

Tall Girl noticed the stainless steel container her mother cradled on her lap as she was going on about the virtues of broadening the mind. No doubt the container had some animal body part. There was quite a number of different eyes in jars of formaldehyde cluttering the walls of her laboratory in the garage at home. Mother had been a geneticist at the university but lost her job there when her research became too controversial. She'd been sacrilegious about the Great Goddess as well. That was definitely a no-no. They gave her a position in food safety testing in the slaughterhouse. Mother didn't talk about it which was strange because she had a long-winded opinion of most things.

"What were you testing today?" Tall Girl said, changing the subject.

"We were processing pigs and monkey meat."

"You took something again?"

"Testicles," Mother whispered.

"What about the bots, mother?"

"They're as dumb as sticks," she said drinking the last of the a-loid, then she lifted up the steel box. "Primates," mother mouthed the word, as her eyes brightened like shimmering black pools.

*   *   *

"It seemed counter intuitive," Teacher said, turning toward the class. "But experience taught us just the opposite. The lower the sperm count, the higher the aggression, bitterness, and desire to punish. And to whom did the demonic patriarchy turn against? The earth loving, peace loving, goddess loving wombs. So we fought back."

Teacher turned again toward the wall screen. A new image appeared. It was a womb with a machine gun.

"This is Karen Endercoff holding the weapon she invented: the Karendercoff. Beautiful, isn't it? Here is a photo of the very largest battalion of warriors. One hundred thousand armed with what?"

"Karendercoffs," said Nicora. "My aunt has one."

"Oh, and so do I. She won her school's competition. Which school?" Teacher brightened another degree.

"T parish."

"Good goddess, that's wonderful. I hope someone in this class wins the shooting competition at the end of term. How many of you are planning to compete? Show of hands?" Since it was mandatory, all the girls raised their hands. "Splendid," Teacher said. "What a plum if someone in my class won. Okay, umm, oh yes, the battles and the victory. It was a slow process, but the phallic weren't prepared for street fighting. That's where the wombs had the advantage. Kill your father, kill your brother was the wombs war cry and it drove terror into the core of the phalli. The final days found them cramped up in one dome. That's what they do, yes, that's what they did. Hide, and rather than die they negotiated a truce, long enough to organize their time travel rockets and leave the planet and never return. Goddess bless us that they don't come back. But we must be prepared. That's why we continue to stay vigilant. Glory to the wombs."

"Glory to the wombs," the class replied in unison.

Tall girl opened her mouth to perform the expected response but a strange idea overwhelmed her. Was Teacher a bot? Were there others, some of her fellow students? Maybe Nicora was a bot, a gone rouge bot who would come to school some day with her auntie's Karendercoff and spray the class with Karendercoff bullets. Too weird. But Teacher, a bot that had a breast reduction. They were still pretty big. Maybe Tall Girl, she, herself was a bot. No, of course not, when cut she bled.

Then she sat up straight. She was having that unfamiliar feeling again. The beginning of her period. She got up with her shoulder bag in tow. In the washroom stall she checked. Sure enough there was a spot of blood on her underwear. She would try the pad this time and peeled off the adhesive strip.

The task completed she sat on the toilet. There was no rush to go back to the class. She tapped a rhythm on the stone tiled floor with her hard soled shoes.

Smile turns up

Frown turns down

This old world goes round and round

Round and round, round and round

Turn the tall girl upside down.

She had a good idea where Teacher would be in her lecture. The phallic obsessive quest for immortality and that would be mortal sin. But if you were immortal would a mortal sin mean diddly squat? Then it would be how the wombs began rebuilding the dome and bigger, better domes and they'd all chant "Keep the earth alive."

And then the last bit where the womb army had the phalli and their FTA (faster than anything) rockets surrounded and the rockets blasting off burning to death hundreds of the wombs bravest and finest fighters. The rockets would disappear into the past or maybe not.

Tall Girl decided to go back to the class, otherwise she'd attract too much attention. She should get there for the scene of the big memorial build for those last fighters and how it was incumbent for all wombs to make pilgrimage at least once in their sweet, short and blessed life.

"And so this is the moment of the dawning of Wenega. Can anyone tell me the derivation of this name? Tall Girl?"

"It's the words new and age spelled backwards."

"Very good. See you all next week."

*　*　*

Mother had taken the whole week off from work to spend time in the workshop lab in the garage. On Friday she watched as her centrifuge whirled to a final halt. Protein chains from the monkey Y chromosome had been incorporated into a sample of Billy Buck's semen. She called out to her bot to join her in the lab.

"Billy Buck, are you charged up?"

"Always my dear."

"Billy Buck, dearest, you've been shooting blanks for a while, how about some live ammo?"

"You've had your five daughters, hot stuff. I'm just a sports model now."

"You still have plenty of active semen in the freezer, macho bot."

"What? I haven't heard I've been reassigned. Have I done something wrong?"

"Nothing worse than usual," she said handing a notepad covered in numbers, letters and illustrations.

"Well, I've never seen this kind of chromosome pattern before. Why do you want to mask the 23rd pair with this funny shaped one?"

"I want to make a phalli."

"No, that's, well, that's kind of crazy. Besides you're infertile now. You stopped making eggs years ago."

"It wasn't that long ago."

Billy Buck's eyes started to flicker. Fertility bots had to use extra power to contemplate time longer than the ovulation cycle.

"Don't blow a fuse darling. It's not me, it's Tall Girl," mother said.

"Woo, that's taboo. It's like infidelity."

"Infidelity, ha. Fidelity has never been your greatest virtue. What about Sash in the bakery and what's her name at the art gallery and I don't know who else."

"Since when did you care about that. Their bots were down and they were prime. Very prime. Beside," he said indignantly. "I'm a Billy Buck after all."

"Indeed you are. That's why you're the bot for the job."

"Tall Girl will have her very own bot very soon. Just wait till she is given her own bot."

"She'll never be allowed her own fertility bot, Billy. She's different. Her eyes, her late puberty, and now, the tonsillectomy business. Tall girl is destined to carry a phallic. Don't you see?"

"My eyes work fine, mother."

"Don't be so literal, you big phoney."

"The different coloured eyes, the tonsils, the destiny. That story is just an old wives tale. Nothing else. Gee."

"Old wives know more than given credit. I think differently than you."

"Yeah, I know that, that's for sure. But I can't initiate congress, that's not allowed for bots. There is no protocol for it."

"She will come to you. She knows the protocol, all girls are taught.

"It's a dumb, dumb, dumb idea, mother. A phallic? Impossible. And monkey sperm? I don't know what to say."

"I know what I'm doing. I know this stuff."

"Hum, maybe," he said with his bot brow furrowed.

"You're jealous, afraid you'll become obsolete. The phallic will usurp you stubborn bots."

"Hum, what I understand about phalli is they don't like to be bossed around, especially by wombs."

"I'm in charge. Correct?"

"Correct my dear. Still, the final decision is Tall Girl's."

"Of course B.B., of course," mother said looking at the electron microscope image. "Oh how beautiful, splendid."

*   *   *

Tall Girl got off the train at L station. The sun was low in the sky and the light cast long shadows. The contrast between light and dark made the colours more vivid than she could ever remember. It was like she had discovered a remarkable secret. Why was there life? Why was there a world? Why was there anything?

She slowly lifted her head to look at the sky's many hues of blue and the thin sliver of moon reflecting bright and beautiful. Outside the dome you could live for a few days, maybe a week, before your lungs, eyes, everything would fail. Inside the dome and underground they could survive. And that survival demanded absolute social cohesion.

"Blessed be the great goddess Wenega," Tall Girl invoked. Then a wave of sadness overcame her as if this ecstasy of just being was a foolish girl womb delusion. She looked at the ground. She was no longer a child, she was a womb. And she would be a childless one at that. What was her purpose in this great collective? The world of fellow wombs.

She walked onward, head bowed in reflection. Soon she recognized the cracks in the side walk in front of the Sip a-loid lunch bar. Looking up she saw the windows shuttered and the door padlocked. A sign on the door read; 'Permanent Closure by Court Order'. Then closer still the smaller text. 'Violation of the Morality, Terrorists and Dissemination of Propaganda Laws'.

Tall Girl returned to the narrow trail that ran beside the overhead rail. She waited and watched as some factory workers stopped to read the signs and then moved on to climb the stairs to the train platform. No one mentioned the a-loid joint as they passed. Don't say anything, don't even think about it, Tall Girl concluded. She began walking. It was nearly November and days were notably shorter. The artificial rain fell lightly although there were no clouds outside the dome. The droplets made a pleasant sound striking the dry leaves as did their crunch under her footsteps.

In school they taught Old Wise Womb sayings. She remembered one of them now. 'The problem is solved by walking around.' The problem was she wasn't sure what the problem was. The more she thought the more muddled her ideas seemed. She had no purpose, and that thought had a solidity to it. Perhaps she did need a purpose. What was her purpose? Ah, the problem. Then she imagined old Karen Endercoff walking alone in the impending nightfall of a cold winter day calculating the solution to her important problem. Why not enter the competition. It was a place to start at least. With practice she could win the Karendercoff. That could be the first step to her purpose.

Billy Buck was preparing dinner when she arrived home.

"Are you hungry, T.G.?" he said.

"Very. I want meat," she replied as she breezed past and into the bathroom. "Good goddess," she whispered, looking at the pad saturated with blood. She replaced it with a fresh one and washed her hands.

"Are you going back to work on Monday?" asked Tall Girl eating the last of her supper.

"Yes," said mother. "Billy Buck, you can clear the table now."

"Good. It's been a whole week of rice and beans, beans and rice. I really need some meat."

"Me too. I'll bring some nice alligator home on Monday. A treat just for you."

"Okay, that would be prefect. I'm pretty tired, I'm bleeding. I'm going to lie down for a while."

"Of course sweetheart. I'd like to come in to your room and talk in a few minutes."

"Sure," Tall Girl said with a hint of caution.

Tall Girl lay on the bed and reviewed some notes from history class. She was daydreaming about the Karendercoff competition when her mother entered the room and sat on the edge of the bed. Her mother proceeded to lay out her plan for Tall Girl to give birth to a phallic.

"Why am I not surprised?" said Tall Girl.

"In about two weeks, you'll be prime. You have time to think about it."

"Okay," the daughter said.

"Okay what?"

"Okay, I'll think about it."

Mother left Tall Girl alone. The daughter reached with a long arm into her shoulder bag for the book Sue Sip had lent her. She'd been reading it every evening all week. The young womb smiled and said the title softly, "Bachelor Cooking and the Art of Seduction." She laughed and yawned, lay the book under the pillow, then turned out the light. She would think about it, no, she had already made up her mind. It was her destiny after all.

What happened with the crows

It was a few minutes after 9 pm on the 10th of June, a Saturday night. Bernadette sat near the window. She watched the last rays of that day paint a brief warm gold on the the cinder block walls of the industrial building below her. Beyond that she saw the city in the bliss of the month of the longest days.

Happily, the clouds and breeze of the afternoon had shielded her west facing bachelor rooms, from the usual baking heat she often endured. No need for the noisy fans and the periodic cold showers. Just sit and restfully watch the changing pastel clouds and patches of robin's egg blue sky. As the light flooded in under the cloud, the horizon reminded her of the folded sheet at the top of the bed. That narrow line of pale peach presented memories of past places and people.

The antics of a trio of crows interrupted her daydream. Their dips-see-doodles seemed like a repeated pattern, a six pointed star. The trio was suddenly replaced by a quartet. This group bobbed up and down like a group of children on a trampoline. Usually a great flock of crows flew over at sunset, perhaps a thousand or more. They would be heading east to their roost at Burnaby Lake after a day of scavenging downtown. Bernadette smiled and waited for more crows to pass. No flock appeared.

Bernadette tried to remember the last time she'd seen the flock. Murder of crows, that's what they are called. She knew a few things about the bird. Natural history was a lifelong hobby and she was sure it had been a long time since she had witnessed the phenomenal wild life display. Perhaps there was an annual cycle of which she was unaware.

She'd often taken comfort in watching their mass fly over head. It was a celebration of the natural world in an otherwise modern industrial setting. She felt a kinship with the crows. Like humans, they were a remarkably successful species. Their success went in tandem with humanity's leftovers.

Crows paid a price for their great numbers. Each mating pair needed a genetically coded amount of treed territory. Their numbers far exceeded the forests available and so only one in ten mated. The rest remained celibate bachelors. She felt a kind of kinship in this notion too. It wasn't as if she hadn't had lover's, she'd had her share and in a way this gave her a sense of superiority over the ubiquitous black bird. But, alone in her perch, looking down at the darkening city, she was missing her great communal family who had always passed overhead. Not knowing what had happened to the handsome crows brought on a recurring dread. Was it another sign of the end of the world?

It was Saturday night and there was a party she'd been invited to. There might be a suitable man there to flirt with.

She checked the time, 10:01. She sighed and left the window and plopped herself in front of her vanity. Going out required getting dolled up a bit. She began a well rehearsed routine. The phone rang.

"Hello."

"Hi Bernadette, it's Larry. I just finished reading your story."

"Oh."

"Yes, well I say, I was a little upset. I was surprised at the character of Mickey. The circumstances make it pretty obvious it was me you were writing about. I mean, by god, that was what, 40 years ago? You make me out to be some brutish Neanderthal. I mean, really."

"Gee, Lawrence, why do you take offence? It's just a story."

"Just a story? Anyone who knew us then would know right away it was me, it was me you were blabbing on about. I mean, if you want to reveal all your youthful experimentation, foibles, whatever, that's your business, but I'd prefer to be left out of it."

"Have you been drinking?"

"What's that got to do with it?"

"Well, you're being awfully aggressive, I mean..."

"Aggressive? What you said, that's aggressive."

"Well, in a way you're just proving my depiction of you."

"Why call me Mickey? Why not be done with it and use my real name for fuck's sake."

"What's that noise?"

"Noise?"

"In the background; music or something?"

"Oh that, there's some stupid street festival. No car day. No, Italian Days. I don't know. Who cares? Just like you to change the subject. Can't take responsibility. Some things never change."

"Well, you're the one who left me. Left me stranded, heartless, on a whim. I was just telling the truth."

"Well, it's a very skewed version of the truth if you ask me. I say you are just mean and vindictive and really, after all these years. Really."

"It just proves how much you hurt me."

"Hurt you? Give me a break. You took up with what's-his-name in no time flat. You did alright."

"What's-his-name? You don't remember his name?"

"Alright, alright, Gavin. What was he, a foot shorter than you and a little dick too I bet."

"Well Larry, I never met anyone with a dick as big as yours."

"Yeah, right."

"I've seen my share. I did the survey, okay? Larry has the biggest. He can also be the biggest dickhead, and the fact that he can't take a harmless, little story about something that happened 40 years ago just proves what a big dick he is."

"I think you're the one that's been drinking."

"So? Sixty-four is a legal age to have a drink or two. And what are you now? seventy, no, seventy in October. Isn't that right? Seventy in October, You would think your skin would have toughened up by now."

"Tough? Well you're no fresh peach."

"Thanks, I didn't know that."

"Sorry."

"No, you're not."

"What do you mean?"

"Sorry isn't part of your psychology. You are oblivious to the people you wound, trample on, use..."

"Oh for god's sake Bernadette. Don't talk stupid."

"See, that just proves it. Heartless, cruel."

"What?"

"Nothing."

"Nothing?"

"Never mind."

"Never mind?"

"You never really loved me, did you?"

"Ah, of course I did. I mean that's a complicated word. May..., I don't know. Things change, friendship, love, we take them for granted when we're young, maybe. Yes. And hopefully, we don't take them for granted when we're old."

"You took me for granted."

"I've taken all my lovers for granted. That's my lesson."

"Neanderthal."

"The Neanderthal gene, that's where the big dick comes from."

"The story is going to be published in Fiddlehead."

"Hopefully nobody will read it."

"Thanks, thanks a lot. That music? Is that zydeco?"

"Zydeco? Christ, I think so. Wait, wait, I've got the schedule right here. Yeah, it's an Acadian band from New Brunswick."

"I'm coming over."

"Coming over?"

"You have beer there?"

"Yeah."

"See you in fifteen minutes."

"You're coming over here?"

"Yes, why not. You like to dance?"

"Ah, well, yeah."

"Okay then, see you soon. Be ready. Bye."

Bernadette lay the phone on the vanity. She leaned close to the mirror for one last examination of her festive face. Satisfied, she stood and fussed a bit with the top of her dress. Perfect. Neanderthals love cleavage.

At the cottage

Grace Valentine sipped a little of her bitter gin. There was no tonic at the seaside cottage so she drank it with water. She had arrived at the cottage in the early morning the day before, with plans to train for an upcoming marathon with her sister, but the sister hadn't arrived. So, Grace sat in a plastic chair on the beach, watching the calm ocean. In the afternoon the day before, she'd seen a south bound tugboat loaded with what appeared to be gravel. This morning she watched an identical barge pass, heading north, riding high in the water.

"Must be empty," she thought.

The barge was a singular reminder of a distant industrial world and it seemed strangely comforting in contrast to the idyllic pleasantries of the location. She thought it was a perfect example of yin and yang. A state of mind her therapist would wax poetic about. Grace raised her drink to view the scene through the distortions of the glass.

"Fuck the therapist," she said as a toast.

A half dozen small pleasure craft were anchored one hundred meters offshore, just beyond the low tide line. The calm sea weakly lapped onto the sandy part of the beach with clumsy rhythm. Grace looked to the southern point of the cove. On the point's barren red sandstone stood a tall pole with a flaccid red and white Canadian flag which pierced the very pale blue sky.

Grace heard voices and turned her head back toward the beach in front of her. There were two small boys, the youngest looked two or three years old. Two women were with them, maybe the mother and grandmother, Grace thought. The children were inspecting the shallow lagoons for treasures, some little crabs, smooth stones or unique shells. The older boy found something interesting and the younger one wanted it. What a howl the small one erupted, and after an eternal minute the mother retreated toward the high ground. The little child's pitch altered, signalling abandonment. His mother abruptly returned to the child and distracted him with a treasure of his own.

Grace viewed the little scene with undivided attention from her plastic beach chair perch. She sat her drink on a huge driftwood log. The tall cedar and Douglas fir trees behind her blocked the early morning sun, leaving her in the cool shadow. The little demon had found some new cause for complaint and was wailing again. The family group now walked carefully over rocks and seaweed away from the water. Grace wondered if they had noticed their only audience and were leaving out of respect for some middle-aged woman's peace and quiet. She felt a moment of guilt at the thought even though she was relieved not to be privy to another tantrum.

Almost instantly she wished they had stayed, because now she was left with her own concerns. Getting rid of the body. She groaned and looked over at her dory resting on the pebbles at the high tide mark. The axe splitting her husband's head now seemed the easy part. That was so swift and precise right here on the beach with the near full moon glistening on the cold steel. The rising tide had washed away the blood. She'd wrapped the body in a canvas sack that lay in the dory. Then she added beach stones to the contents of the sack. More than enough to make the whole affair sink to the ocean floor, she had calculated. She wondered now about cutting open his abdomen so his body wouldn't bloat.

The death was quick, but the business of luring him to the beach and filling the bag with body and rocks took longer than she thought. Her plan was simple enough. Row the dory out to the motor boat anchored 100 meters away. The sack was too heavy for her to shift, but the winch on the motor boat would do just fine. By the time the dory was ready to cast off the tide was receding and the weight of the lousy bastard had the dory resting on the beach. She had pushed and grunted and pulled and cried, but the damn dory wouldn't budge.

That was an eternal six hours ago and she had been on the beach ever since. In six more hours the tide would be full again. At 2:03 pm, on this good day of our lord she could row the dory to the seventeen foot, fiberglass watercraft. The boat with Grace's maiden name written in stylish cursive on the bow. Its powerful ninety horsepower motor would speed the Grace Valentine with dory in tow out into the middle of the Strait. Then she'd winch the dearly departed dead weight over the side. Grace pictured the bag dropping deeper and deeper into the dark world below.

"No, no, no, no."

It was the small child again, with the grandmother, who was exercising great patience. Grace thought the kid needed a good whack. Not an axe through the head, mind you, but some corporal discipline. The grandmother's demeanour was not lost on Grace. Her comportment was worthy of emulation in fact. Perhaps the child had one of those mental affections where they suffered great alienation and were unable to communicate in a normal way. She decided not to stare and the duo slowly zigzagged away down the beach. Grace tried to administer the grandmother's calm on herself. She thought about her breathing and her thoughts slowed. She'd been keeping vigil on the beach all night and for what purpose? No one was going to steal the bag of body and stones. She could go back to the cottage and sleep. Sleep? She couldn't sleep. Hell no. Of course there was TV. Maybe watch a space adventure or someone renovating a kitchen or some sport thing. They called it the boob-tube for a reason.

She heard a noise, a hissing. Grace imagined a sea serpent. She turned, looking around. It was the automatic sprinklers at the vacant summer home next to the cottage. According to the women at the gas station the residence had ten bedrooms and sat empty fifty weeks of the year. The world didn't make sense. Killing Stan was the start of it making sense.

The sun had cleared the trees behind her and she could feel its warmth on the back of her head. She had cut her long thick hair short the day before and she wondered about getting her ears sunburned. There was sunscreen in the cottage. She stood up and immediately sat down again. Gravity was too great.

"Christ."

Grace willed herself up, went to the cottage, and put on a wide-brimmed hat. This delay would have a ripple effect. There was Stan's stuff to get rid of. There wasn't much, but she felt dirty with it around. She stuffed his clothes into a plastic bag and put them into the trunk of the car. On the beach she could see a stout woman looking into the dory.

"Hey," yelled Grace and slammed the trunk. The woman looked toward Grace. Then Grace lurched toward the beach but was held in place. She screamed before she realized the hem of her smock was caught by the closed trunk. The fat lady was on the run now, glancing back hoping the crazy redhead wasn't chasing her. Mrs. Valentine ripped her shirt from the trunk and lurched robotic-like back into the cottage. As she wandered from room to room the silence calmed her. In the kitchen she opened the refrigerator. There was Stan's beer. Grace took one, drank the whole thing, and laughed. Stan wasn't going to need it. She opened another and stood at the kitchen window watching the beach and the dory. She placed the cold can against the warm skin of her face and neck. Her boyish haircut had worked its charm on her husband. Deceased husband. Grace smiled and closed her eyes.

The bastard had a thing for young men. He wooed and married her to please his square-ass family and his inheritance. He liked her physique, slim in the hips and flat chested. She didn't care for anal sex but she did her giving wife thing. Thankfully he had a little dick. It didn't matter now, big dick, little dick, she'd be in charge now. Men had always been attracted to her after all. She had charm, wit, intelligence, beauty, drive. Why she chose Stan baffled everyone. He was a good cook, literary and arty, but he was also a mean, cruel drunk and he was drunk plenty. For ten years she had tried to shape him but he wasn't clay. He'd been cast solid long before she'd met him, and he was a liar. A liar to her, and a liar to himself, afraid to come out of the closet. But the new haircut seduced him big time.

"Come down to the beach, Stan sweetie, and I'll suck you off," she had told him.

He came along like a lapdog and she knelt on the sand in the moonlight. She washed his hard-on with salty water and he laughed at the sensation. Grace didn't want to remember the taste of his little cock. She pretended it was somebody else, anybody else, maybe the man at the gas station or her Korean acupuncturist.

Stan was rough with her and she said she was delighted. He was about to shoot his pathetic little load when she stood tall, reached into the dory and picked up the axe. The look on his face. Grace felt a moment of delight, how she now cherished that stunned expression. It surprised her how easily the axe penetrated his skull. And death came so quickly. Poisoned prisoners on death row suffer longer.

Grace opened her eyes. Had the waterline moved? Was it coming in? Yes , yes, yes. She took a swig of beer. Grace Valentine never drank beer, hardly ever anyway. Didn't care for it. It wasn't bad, first thing in the morning. Wasn't there a song about that?

"The beer I had for breakfast wasn't bad, so I had one more for dessert," she sang.

That's right, she thought. It was a country song. Stan hated country music. That was it, Stan's requiem. Grace located her Ipod. There was a setting for classic country.

"God bless us, a bunch of them."

Grace listened to the lyrics. 'Oh, the snakes crawl at night, that's what they say. When the sun goes down then the snakes will play'.

Grace put Stan's variety pack of beer into a cooler and carried it out to beach. She propped up a shade umbrella and settled into a white plastic lawn chair. She remembered her father liked this kind of music. He liked all kinds of music, but he didn't think highly of Stan. He never said much of anything negative, only, "You're old enough to make your choices."

Grace hadn't been there when her father died. She'd been studying and working on a paper; Surrealists Poetry and Political Action. Christ. She hadn't thought about that for a while. But her father's death was sudden and she'd wished she'd seen him before he died. He was the real deal. Marlboro man without the tobacco. He'd been her model for what a man was supposed to be and had projected that image on those who didn't deserve the ownership. Her naive mind of youth stayed stubbornly resilient. By the time she had met Stan she should have known better.

Grace had a long drink of beer. Some of the brew ran down her chin and she dabbed her jaw with the back of her dry hand. She could acquire a taste for the beverage. The can's label was an attractive mountain scape. The brew was very filling too.

"To life."

There were twenty or more people scattered around the small cove now. Two teenage boys with water skimming boards were flitting across the shallow sea surface. She thought their agility and cockiness were glorious. They would be around Luke's age. Her adopted son's age when he committed suicide. Time stood still for an instant. He was always with her, always would be. Safe and strong and pure always in her memory. That was a sacred realm. That realm had a special emotion, self righteous vengeance.

Grace could not prove it, but she believed Stan had violated a fundamental trust. Touched their son, used him, spoiled him, had sex with him. Fucked up the boy's gentle mind, drove him to such despair that he'd taken his own life. But now justice was complete and the resurrection of her son would eventually form eternal and exquisite in her memories. Only the good would remain, the bad would become covered in silt and a couple hundred meters of cold sea brine. Buried forever and forgotten.

The tide was coming in. Yes, one could actually see it move across the sand flats. Soon it would meet the rock and seaweed, then the small smooth pebbles up the slight grade to her bright white dory.

'Hey good-lookin', what ya got cookin?'

How's about cookin' somethin' up with me?'

Tears trailed her cheeks and her hands shook as Grace wrestled another brew from the cooler. She forced herself to quietly sing along.

"Got a hot rod Ford and a two dollar bill,

I know a spot right over the hill,

There's soda pop and the dancin' is free.

If you wanta' have fun come along with me.'

"Grace, Grace Valentine. Hello. How are you?"

She looked toward the distant point where the flag waved gently. Then she focused at the dory. A man stood beside it waving in her direction.

"Sta...."

"Hey, is that you Grace?"

No, she realized. It wasn't Stan. The man was too big, too dark. She sat upright, drew a deep breath and held it.

"It's me Carlos. Remember me? You remember me, Carlos?"

"Carlos... yes... Carlos."

Who was this man? He walked toward her and she recognized the long graceful stride.

"Your name is on the boat," he said.

"Yes."

He was close enough to judge her condition. She appeared to be loaded. Then her face formed into a glorious smile. Her body relaxed and knees of her long legs fell apart. The red fabric of her red bathing bikini clinging to her contours. Memories of that particular part of her anatomy flooded back as Carlos felt a happy surge in his own groin. Her hair is red down there too, he recalled.

"How are you?" he said.

Grace just nodded.

"This is such a beautiful spot," he continued.

"I'm celebrating."

"I see."

He placed a plastic chair beside her and opened up the shade umbrella that stood sentinel between them. She held up her left hand and pointed at its wedding band.

"He's gone. Stan, he's gone. Beer? Cold."

"Sure."

"He was in Indonesia. He's a doctor, Stan is. The company he worked for were building a pulp mill in the middle of a big forest there. Everybody lives in a big compound. All the foreigners, the workers, Brits, Canadians, Americans, engineers, all that. The army patrols the perimeter to keep the locals down. The lower office staff come from the cities. You know the young Indonesian girls. They work and live in the compound too. He met one of them. His new child bride. Its common, old white guys pairing up with pretty...whatever."

"I'm sorry."

"I don't care. She can have him. He wasn't much of a lover. Not like other men I've known"

She put her hand on his forearm and continued.

"Enough about me, what's the handsome Carlos been up to?"

Carlos talked for a long time covering the span of twenty five years since the last time they had seen each other. They laughed and drank beer. Grace mostly listened and soon she remembered how much he liked to talk. It was nice to have the company and the distraction. At times she was just listening to the sound and watching his movement. Carlos was a devotee of flirting and Grace played gracious and coy.

"You're shooting a movie, on the other side of that point."

"Yes indeed Grace. Its a big day tomorrow. I came up this morning. The motel in town is nice. I have my fitting tonight. My Santa suit."

"Santa?"

"Playing Santa again. Ha. I don't need any padding. But hey, its a couple days, maybe three, I'm hoping so anyway. The location supposed to be Hawaii. Sort of, looks a bit like it, here. It's kind of a science fiction script, you know, with aliens. Everybody in the world has been captured by the aliens except this small group on a remote island, and these people are... they are trying to live a normal life, celebrating Christmas, like they used too. At the same time they are trying to free all the other earthlings."

"Free the earthlings, right on."

"You look real good, Grace, real good."

"Oh, Carlos, you're so sweet, but tell me, tell me about the movie. It sounds so fun."

"Well okay, the aliens, they came here a long time ago."

"Came from where?" Grace said.

"Outer space?" They both laughed. "And they landed in the ocean and lived under the sea floor, for hundreds of years. But, as the ah, the oceans got more polluted the aliens started getting sick and dying off."

"Uh, huh, okay."

"They realized it was the humans that were poisoning the ocean, so they came out of the water in their big space ship and started capturing and killed many humans. But, but the aliens are divided on what to do with the humans. One group of aliens wants to kill off all the humans, while the other ones want to teach the humans how to survive without destroying the ocean. And the people. Well they are divided too, some want to fight the aliens and some want to try to make peace with them.

"Santa is an alien?" Grace said.

"Ha, I wish, I might get more days, but no, Santa is a human. I'm just a human. At first Santa thinks he should join the humans who are attacking the aliens but then he has a change of heart and he joins in with the people who want to learn from the aliens. And, well, basically it's Santa, the spirit of Christmas who will finally bring them all together."

"So, you have a big part, Carlos."

"No, just seven lines. But it's, I think it's a pivotal part."

"And that's the movie then?"

"Well, there's more, but I haven't read the whole script. I'm just a day player. They only give me the scenes I'm in. But, this part I really like. The really cool thing is they built the big space ship, and it's big, really big. Like football field in size and at least three stories high. They are supposed to pull it up here today. With tugboats, three tugboats. One in front, two in the back. It will pass by right here."

Grace followed the line of Carlos' hand toward the ocean. The tide was nearly full and the waves were splashing against the bow of the dory.

"Oh, Carlos, can you help me push the dory into the water?" she said.

Grace slipped a smock over her muscular shoulders, went to the dory and sat the cooler far from the bag. Carlos followed her.

"I need to go out to the motor boat."

"You sure?" said Carlos.

"Absolutely."

Carlos pushed the dory till the bow was afloat. She wrapped her arms tightly around him.

"You're my hero," she said.

Then she climbed in the dory, he shoved her free and she began to row.

"Come see me again," she called to him.

"Be careful, Grace."

He stood on the shore and watched her pull into the oars. The ship-lapped wooden dory lay out a narrow wake. Then he remembered, she was a competitive rower at college. He smiled, Grace hadn't lost her form. Carlos waved and turned toward the point where the flag fluttered in the steady wind.

Grace was winded when she tied the dory to the motor boat's stern. Then she splashed her face in the water. The sensation was invigorating and the exertion gave her enough renewed bravado to jump into the water. The idea of sitting in the dory with the rigid body any longer seemed undignified. She swam along the motor launch's starboard side, round the bow and down the port side. Then she reversed direction back to the starboard. The ritual inspection of the craft complete, she grasped the ladder positioned there and pulled herself aboard.

Grace aggressively tried to start the engine. Too much throttle and the engine sputtered and died. She waited, allowing the excess fuel to evaporate and then turned the ignition key. The engine coughed then smoothly fell into a contented cheetah purr. The Grace Valentine pulled anchor and slowly the boat moved away from the shore. Her skipper couldn't look back for fear of seeing Stan standing in the dory pissing over the side. When she finally did, all she saw was the dory weave back and forth like a sleepy cow's tail within the confines of the motor crafts wake. She smiled, plucked a beer and drank a long refreshing gulp.

The headwind was steady as Grace aimed the boat toward the gap between two islands. The smaller island to the south was called Merry, the larger one to the north was Thormanby. It would be an hour before she would pass between the islands and then another hour before getting to the center of the Strait. She checked the fuel and there was plenty. Far enough from shore not to be seen, Grace hung the wet smock up to dry in the sun and wind and removed her wet bikini top which she lay on the hot deck. She correctly imagined herself Amazonian at the helm. Life was good. She removed the bottom half of her bikini. She was surprised to see blood. It was her blood. She was menstruating.

"Christ, I though this damn business was over."

She hadn't had a period since before last Christmas. Grace counted the months. Nine months. Grace put the boat in neutral and opened the first aid kit. There was a small transparent container with her name on. She didn't recognize the name of the drug. Who gives a shit, it was empty anyway. She couldn't find the napkins. Stan must have removed the little packet of sanitary napkins. She stomped naked to the stern of the boat and yelled at the dory.

"You bastard, you fucking bastard."

She noticed a few drops of blood on the deck. She had left a little trail. God, this was full blown, this was the real thing. Grace began to laugh. She bent over with laughter with her hands on her face. She laughed so hard she began to cry, then she stopped and went back to the first aid box and fashioned a napkin out of gauze. She cleaned herself and fitted the makeshift pad into the half dry bikini bottoms and slid them on. Then she put on the drying smock and took the helm.

The boat had drifted a bit but Grace renewed the course. The Grace Valentine was within a half kilometer of the channel when she saw it. Two tugs south down the strait. Then behind just appearing into view from behind Thormanby Island was what had to be the alien space ship. They were against the current, so they weren't moving fast. She guessed the tugs would keep south once they rounded Merry Island. Her only option was to lay in wait or motor north around Thormanby Island. She turned north full throttle. Grace felt both confused and empowered by the return of her period. Was she some phoenix rising? Was she returning to her youth? Forty minutes later she rounded the north end of Thormanby Island. The seas were rough here but she keep the speed up and was soon into calmer water about half way down the west face of the island. Grace was about to turn out into deeper water when she glanced to the rear. Her heart fluttered. Where was the dory? She'd lost the dory. Oh, my god.

The Grace Valentine back tracked. The tide was pushing toward the island so she kept her lookout to the north-east. After a very long fifteen minutes she saw the craft very close to the shore. She motored in as close as possible and dropped anchor. Then she stripped naked, dove in and swam the 30 meters to the dory. Grace tied its rope around her waist and swam on her back toward the boat. It was a slow business. When she finally reached the boat she tied up, climbed aboard and lay on the deck numb. The heat of the day was spent as the sun went behind the dark cloud resting on the western horizon. There were three beer in the cooler. Then there were two. The sugar and alcohol gave Grace the spirit of energy to get her on her feet. She dried the best she could and dressed. As much as she disliked the idea, she had better lift the bagged corpse aboard. Grace fastened the hydraulic winch cables to the canvas coffin. At the helm she engaged the winch's clutch and slowly lifted the cargo from the dory to the boat deck.

The sun set as the alien space ship returned to its own cove down the southern coast. She was cold as the boat roared out toward open water. After a half hour she stopped. Not far away the large car ferry passed with its many lights a blazing. Grace waited until it was far away before winching the cargo over the side and it hung there barely touching the water. She opened a can of beer and took a swig.

"Would you like a beer Stan, a little sip before you go? What's that? I can't hear ya. I can't Stan, you'll have to speak up. Ha, ha. The ol' silent treatment huh? At a loss for words are ya? The beer's mighty tasty. Umm. Oh, what the heck, have a little taste." She poured some beer onto the hanging bag.

"Gee Stan, I can't believe you would let good beer go to waste. Gee, you really must be dead. Dead and going, going …," Grace cut the rope and the bag disappeared into the dark waters. "Gone."

The Grace Valentine headed east with the wind and tide pushing her forward. As she slid dead center between the dark lumps of Thormanby and Merry islands she remembered how they got their names. British sailors in the 1860's had placed a bet on a horse named Thormanby, owned by a man named Merry and it had won them a fine payout. The erratic current between the islands gave the little craft a wild exhilarating ride. Once through, the inner coastal waters were much calmer.

The full moon rose over the mainland playing peek-a-boo with the passing clouds while below a string of lights indicated the line of cottages. The point was distinctive with its white light shining up on the flag and its pole. Grace guessed where the cottage was in relation to the point. It was just a matter of time and she'd be ashore and making ready to sleep alone and happy in the quaint little seaside home. She yawned.

"Stay awake dear, stay awake."

She yawned again, hearing the low steady rhythm of the engine and rocking to the gentle peaks and valleys of the calm ocean. Grace felt sure dead reckoning was correct. She sang and pushed the throttle to full.

"As, I was a walking down Cordova Street. Way, hey, blow the man down.

A handsome young laddie I happened to meet. Way, hey, blow the man down."

Goldie Goldonski, a young and pretty RCMP constable was standing on the front deck of the Valentine cottage. Her large brown eyes scanned the sea with binoculars. She could hear the conversation that her superior officer, Charles Laplace was having with Dr. Valentine and the doctor's son, Luke.

"She's been drinking and she's not taken her medication," the doctor said.

"Your wife was alone, no one was with her," said Charles.

"Yes, her sister was supposed to arrive two days ago but her flights got diverted because of those damn drones. She's not expected till later tonight. She wouldn't arrive here till mid day tomorrow at the earliest. They were planning to run the marathon next week. "

"Marathon, really," said the policeman.

"Shouldn't we call the coast guard? I mean, the boat's gone," said Luke.

"Yes, I agree."

"I've notified them already sir," said Goldonski, still scanning, although the clouds now obscured the moonlight.

After a short while the Grace Valentine began to veer off course. Grace was slumped over the her name sake's wheel. The little craft was heading nearer the point than the cottage.

The three men heard Goldonski's voice again. "A small craft coming in near the point, Sergeant. It's moving very fast."

The quartet ran down the beach. It was a hell of a racket when the Grace Valentine hit the beach. The engine stalled and the vessel listed on a forty five angle. Grace awoke in the salt water not sure who or where she was. Her face, forearms and knees were scratched and stinging from contact with the barnacled rock a half meter beneath the water line. She scrambled ashore by instinct and headed down the beach in the right direction by luck rather than judgment.

"Sergeant, I think we've found her."

The moon broke through the clouds and Luke brought his mother inside and cleaned and bandaged her wounds.

"I grounded the boat near the point," she said and cried.

The two police officers said goodnight and got into their cruiser.

"The grounded vessel is named after her?"

"Yes," answered Goldonski.

They notified the coast guard of the location of the Grace Valentine. The coast guard would secure it and inspect the damage. The cops sat quietly for a moment looking out at the water and the reflection of the moon upon it.

"It really is beautiful here," said Goldonski.

"Yes, especially with the moon. It brings out all the crazies."

"He's a nice man," Goldie said.

"The doctor?"

"Yes, and the son too."

"Are you working tomorrow, security on the movie shoot?" asked Charles.

"Double time, I suppose I should. Are you?" she said.

"Oh yeah, that pretend stuff, I love it. Such a nice break from reality."

"I suppose it is. We need to write a report tonight on this Grace Valentine thing?" she asked.

"No, not tonight. We can do it tomorrow on set. You known, during the hurry up and wait part. Everything seems to be under control. It's low tide just after dawn. I'll come by in the morning and examine the boat first thing. I'll talk to the Valentine's, if they're awake. Coast Guard will be here early. I expect it to be routine. Otherwise...."

"Otherwise, what sir?"

"Oh, it really is beautiful here," he sighed.

"Yes, very. Some people are so lucky," she said and watched a cloud slowly pass in front of the moon. "Shall we go Charles?"

"Yes, lets leave this paradise before we never will."

She started the engine. The wheels crunched along on the gravel driveway, then up and out of sound and sight of the placid sea and into the great, dark forest

The Dreamer

"The boy's a dreamer, Mrs. Green. That's fine some of the time, but schoolwork and well, the rigours of life in general demands focus and concentration, discipline, self-discipline."

The teacher slid her glasses back on her nose and looked down at her notes. The mother, Mrs. Green sat quietly, her hands folded on her lap. She felt like a child herself in the face of authority. Mrs. Winchester continued.

"He's good at music and okay in math, but spelling and well....," the teacher paused for effect as she looked up at the pale thin woman.

Mrs. Green wanted to unload her life history, but instead she pretended to be completely attentive to the round, short, grey-haired old biddy. She'd like to say, she wasn't a misses at all. She was a miss. Her son's father was a bass player she'd slept with once. He went by the name of Bingo, that's what the other members of the band called him, Bingo, and that is what he said when he gave her an orgasm. It had been the first time she'd had an orgasm with somebody else.

"Is something funny, Mrs. Green?"

"No Mrs. Winchester. I was thinking about Rodney's father. He's a musician," she said and vocalized a funky bass line.

"Maybe that's where he gets his ear for music and rhythm," Mrs. Green added.

"Ah hum."

"I love music, anything with a good beat. You know what I mean? Like Elvis said, 'its gotta' move me man'. Right?"

"Right."

"I like classical too, the Russian stuff, even the spooky kind. How about you?"

"Oh, hum, well. I'm very fond of music. I listened to a lot of folk music, Joni Mitchell, but your son, his attentiveness. We need to encourage that aspect of learning. Perhaps he spends too much time with his father, his father's vocation."

Mrs. Green blinked and nodded and clenched her hands a little tighter. Mrs. Winchester looked at her watch. These parent-teacher pow-wows were an evil exercise. She took a deep breath in a salute to her own professionalism, glanced at her notes and then at the parent.

The woman had an appealing figure. She'd always liked the home team herself, but when she got married to Harold, she took his name and played the straight girl. He was good about it, so sweet really, shaved his body smooth and put on a little lace and garter belt. Still, it wasn't the female form. It was more than breasts and hips, it was presence, attitude, vulnerability.

She was the type Mr. Winchester seemed to be interested in of late. They were professional, that is, actors in porn films. Often scrawny from drugs: speed or coke or something. After twenty years of marriage her husband showed up with a woman for both of them. It was great when he'd watch while she'd get it on with some young thing, all perky and well, kind of naive just like Mrs. Green. It kept the home fires burning.

Watching him screw them wasn't really her thing, still it was instructive and well, the lord giveth and the lord taketh away. In the great scheme of things, life was good. Still, she seemed always to be the follower and never the leader, the one to react rather than initiate.

"What can I do to help my son improve his grades?" said Mrs. Green.

"What?" Mrs. Winchester replied.

"My son?"

"Oh, sorry. You're the last parent-teacher conference tonight. I must be tired."

The teacher smiled for the first time and Mrs. Green undid the tight bun of hair on the back of her head.

"I tried to help with his project, but, like I know diddly squat 'bout Greek myths."

The woman's hair rested like fingers on her broad shoulder. The teacher noticed the mother had the neck, and chin and mouth of her son. Mrs Winchester suddenly felt as if she'd been pierced by an arrow. She thought of Hera instructing Cupid to shoot his arrow at Medea. Medea instantly fell in love with the hero, Jason. Was Mrs. Green her hero?

"I'm sure we can improve your son's grade point average. Work toward a scholarship at a good music school. He has a voice, a voice of an angel," she put her hand over Mrs. Green's hand with its thin gold ring. "Mr. Green, does he have a big influence on his son?"

"Not really," said Mrs. Green.

"I like him, your son. And I like his mother."

Mrs Winchester watched as Mrs Green leaned over and kissed the teacher's hand.

"I like the Russian alphabet," said Mrs. Green.

Mrs Winchester furrowed her brow.

"The letters of the Russian alphabet. Here, I'll show you." Mrs Green wrote out the letters on a piece of paper.

"They are beautiful," sighed Mrs. Winchester.

Mrs Green stood and lifted her skirt and slid off her underwear. The teacher could see the woman wore a small tattoo just above her pubic hair line. She leaned forward for a better look. It was a hammer and sickle between two Kalashnikov machine guns.

"Practice makes perfect," the parent said.

"Oh my dear sweet, Mrs. Green."

Mrs Winchester stood and walked around the desk. She pressed her groin firmly against Mrs. Green's thigh while her stubby fingers gently explored the flesh below the tattoo.

"You have a beautiful mouth Mrs. Green, I want to taste it."

"Give me your tongue, Mrs. Winchester."

The tips of their tongues fenced and Rodney's mother trembled as her companion's fingers ventured inside her.

"You really want it, don't you?" Mrs. Winchester whispered.

"Ah huh."

The teacher stepped back, the parent suspended on her fingertips. She was the puppet master and the authority was intoxicating.

"The alphabet," Mrs. Green said.

"What about the alphabet?"

"Write the letters with your tongue down there."

Mrs Winchester held the paper with the Russian alphabet and knelt in front of Mrs. Green. A twinge of pain in her left knee was intense. It was an old field hockey injury. She could take it for the team. The letters were interesting to make but difficult to remember. Given the engrossing spectacle of Mrs. Green's waves of ecstasy she could be forgiven her lapses of memory. She was just starting to get it on the sixth time through when Mrs. Green's soprano sang, "Bingo!" The flushed pale woman slumped back into the visitor's chair.

Mrs. Winchester's head rested on Mrs. Green's lap. She moved her jaw back and forth relaxing the tensed muscles in her neck. Her partial plate was loose again. It had been doing that, off and on, for a while. She was grateful for her union's good dental plan and must remember to get the work done soon. Mrs. Winchester's eyes watered up and a single tear ran down to the tip of her nose to be absorbed by the fabric of Mrs. Green's skirt.

Rodney opened his eyes and sat up on the edge of his bed. His thirteen-year-old boy's erection stood up in the cold air of his room like the big cannon on a battleship. The idea of his grade eight teacher having sex with his mother disturbed him. He shook his head, hoping to shake the dream away. It worked a little.

Rodney wrapped a towel around his waist, went to the bathroom and urinated. He slowly became flaccid enough to put on his underwear. Back in his bedroom he closed the book on the Cyrillic alphabet, then looked at the history list from the previous evening's online computer browsing. Funky bass lines and girl on girl action were the dominant themes. A click of the clear history option eliminated the evidence of the forbidden.

The young Master Green took five contemplative steps to the second floor window. Below he could see his mother in an old coat wandering about the snow-covered garden. She had her arms folded across her chest and held a steaming cup of coffee in one hand. He watched her make fresh tracks on the fallow earth and then, as if on cue, she turned and looked up at him. His mother smiled and waved and made an eating gesture. He nodded and put his hands on the glass. She could see his pale flawless torso and in her mind she could hear his voice as he mouthed the words.

"Morning Mum."

The landlord

There was a knock on Reg's door. He looked up from his book toward the window beside the basement suite door. He couldn't see anyone, they must be very close to the door. Reg yawned and dropped his feet from the coffee table to the floor. It was a small suite, just a few steps before he opened the door.

"I don't want you having a cat down here, you understand. No male cat spraying in the corners, on the rug. You can never get rid of that stink. I want that cat gone before the end of the week."

Reg had never seen his gay, flight attendant landlord so angry. "Okay," said Reg and tried to shut the door. The French-Canadian landlord whipped up his arm to keep it open. He wasn't finished with his tirade. Reg weathered some more abusive ranting from the man with the bushy mustache and feathered bangs.

"Hey man, the cat's not here, he's gone, okay," Reg said sternly. Andre looked a bit taken aback, but then he appeared not quite ready to abandon his macho pose.

"He better be. I won't stand for pets. It's in the lease."

"What about Maurice and his old dog that shits in the back yard?" Reg pointed overhead. He was referring to the tenant on the main floor between Reg's basement suite and Andre's third floor apartment.

"He's a friend of mine. He's had that dog for twelve years." Andre balanced his hands on his hips as if he was about to make a ballet move. His self-serving sneer abandoned any pretense. Reg knew that the two French-Canadians were long time friends and that Maurice was gay to boot. They often presented as if they belonged to a more highly evolved form of western male culture.

The fact that Maurice ran a 'gourmet' hot dog cart down in Stanley Park and listened to opera was proof of that. The balding, pot bellied Maurice also had a crush on his barely old enough employee, a young Brit with no work visa but plenty of youth and beauty. The old house's lack of soundproofing let Reg know the young man had a passion for doing drag and generally had Maurice around his well manicured little finger.

"Well, you should tell him to clean up the dog shit more often. I'm getting tired of doing it," said Reg.

Andre went up on his toes. "I'm happy with him. He pays his rent on time, all the time. That's more than I can say for you. And I'm getting tired of you being late. I could have you evicted, you know that, don't you?"

Reg sighed. It was true about the rent and it was due again in three days and he knew for a fact that he couldn't pay it all on time again this month. "You'll get your rent," Reg said while adding in thought only, 'when I get it'. Then he said. "Andre, while you're here maybe you could look at the pipe going to the bathtub. There seems to be a leak."

Andre's face scrunched up like a dry potato. At the sight of the landlord's distress, a feeling of glee bubbled up through

Reg's humiliation. "A leak? What did you do?" Andre said and stepped inside and headed for the bathroom. Reg casually followed, finding Andre leaning over the cast iron tub. There was a plastic ice cream container on the floor that caught the drip which fell from a junction in the copper pipe. "Shit, I'll have to call a plumber now, damn."

"Takes about three days before the thing fills up. It's bound to get worse," said Reg.

"It will be fine for now. Maybe put some tape around it. I can't afford to call a plumber today."

"Tape, really, tape?"

"I need to buy some tape, I'll get that today. We'll just shut off the water to the shower for now." With that Andre turned the valve nearest the drip. The ancient casting burst and a fierce spray of water shot up hitting Andre square in the face. He lurched up striking his head on the linen shelf. The flimsy partial board unit came apart and fell lopsided cracking the cover of the ceramic water tank. Andre slipped on the wet floor and he fell against the tub firmly on his chin. The cast iron tub rung a sustained contemplative note as the landlord fell freely to the floor.

Reg watched the remarkably brief performance with a cruel amusement. After a few more seconds he said. "Andre, are you alright?" There was no answer and the water pressure subsided. Reg could now hear Maurice taking a shower directly above him. Reg knelt to take a closer look. Andre's face was cupped by the plastic container; his mouth and nose completely submerged in the cloudy pink water. Reg stood a moment and contemplated the situation. Save one of his fellow human beings or let the prick drown? It shocked him that the latter choice was the preferred one. He stepped to the door sill before his shoes got wet while he unrepentantly concocted a story in his mind. He imagined himself talking to two female paramedics, youthful, beautiful and earnest, captivated by his earthy charms.

"The landlord came to check the plumbing and I went to Patels, to buy a samosa. I do that often, two or three times a week. I checked out the recordings of East Indian movie soundtracks and discussed some of the new releases with Mr Patel. He's a cool guy who's a real aficionado. After that I went to the Napoli coffee. It's beside Patels and got a half pound of their 'family blend.'"

He could show them the coffee. "Smell the Italian roast" he might say. "I was out for less than a half an hour. Then I found him with his face in the water, you know. So I phoned 911 and then did CPR."

Maybe even mouth to mouth on the swishy fag. Now that was an endorsement for compassion. Of course he'd be wise not to say anything offensive about the pompous prick. He watched Andre. The landlord wasn't moving. Perhaps 45 seconds had elapsed. The man's firm bum was stuck up in the air. Perhaps it would be better if the paramedics saw him in this position. He also noticed the bulge of his wallet. He could rob him and then call 911. No, that was stupid. Still it was tempting. The CPR was the safer idea.

Upstairs, Maurice usually took long showers, often using up all the communal hot water. Whatever, let him. The up side was the leak in his suite was reduced to a trickle. He could leave Andre in the water for five or seven minutes. However long it took to avoid death, but induce brain damage. That idea seemed completely awful. Besides the landlord might become a ward of the state, a burden, an unnecessary fate for all involved. No, death was a merciful virtue, short and bitter-sweet, rendering a deep transcendent grief. A noble death. He had always been opposed to the suffering of animals. Putting the beast out of its misery was the moral high ground.

Reg's moment of faux self righteousness was brief. The longer he considered the nuance of the problem, the longer his movement out the door was delayed. Of course, he could assist the fallen man. Still, Reg remained, not moving. Standing still was an option too, except it was a lousy alibi.

It must have been over two minutes, perhaps close to three now and it was decided. He would go and get one of Patels excellent samosas and follow through with the rest of the plan. He turned his back on the washroom, walked through the small kitchen, into the living room and grasped the door knob. It wouldn't turn. Reg held his breath and suddenly felt faint. It took a long moment to diagnose the situation. The dead bolt was unlocked but the door knob wasn't. Reg never used that lock because it was broken and it couldn't unlocked from the inside. Andre must have given it a twist when he came in. "Damn." He had mentioned it a few times but Andre always said. "Yes, I know. Just use the dead bolt."

It could be unlocked from the outside, which meant going out through the window. It also meant that first, Reg would have to find that particular key because he had removed it from his key chain. He was starting to panic. There were keys in the tool drawer and he began searching. "Ohh no, no." Then he thought; Andre might have one in his pocket. The guy was probably dead already. Reg felt dizzy. He wondered if he was going to get sick. He picked up a hammer. Underneath it was the key. "Yes, yes, sweet Jesus, yes." He turned toward the door and sorted through the next steps. Go out the window, unlock the door, go to Patels, get a samosa. "Go out the window, unlock the door, go to Patels, get a samosa. Go out the window, then unlock the door, go to Patels, get a samosa" he whispered the mantra.

"Ahhhhh, uggg," came an animal sound from the bathroom.

"Oh no,"said Reg returning to the bathroom. He witnessed Andre struggle to his feet. They stared at each other.

"Mais pourquoi diable me fait ca?"stammered Andre, who didn't look so good.

"What?" shrugged Reg.

"You hit me with a hammer?"

"You better sit down," Reg said, pointing the hammer at the toilet. "We need to turn off the main water valve, wherever that is?"

"Laundry room," Andre said, still looking at the hammer.

Reg went out the window, unlocked the door and proceeded to the laundry room. He followed the pipe from the hot water heater to what was the main intake. Fortunately the main valve had been upgraded in the not so distance past and the apparatus worked flawlessly. Almost instantly a litany of francophone blasphemies was trumpeted from Maurice, the gourmet hot dog man. "Sacrament! Tabarnac! Criss!"

Reg smiled as he surveyed the asymmetric cobweb of copper and plastic pipes. Then he heard Maurice stomping barefoot on the floor above him. His dog started to bark which made Reg smile more broadly. The old house contained a circus of makeshift repairs and now they would be without running water for a day or two. It was a small price to pay for the faint glimmer of satisfaction he was feeling. Besides with the inconvenience of no water what's the big deal about being a few days late with the rent? It seemed like a perfect moment to celebrate with a tasty samosa.

Weed

Elliot didn't feel well. The discomfort was mostly in his stomach, the whole digestive tract really. Maybe it was the medication. His friend Jane told him he was astrologically fated to have health problems in that part of his body. Jane was a strong believer in the secrets of stars. She also predicted a long and loving relationship between Raisha and himself. Wrong, wrong, wrong. So much for celestial alignments.

He had smoked some weed about fifteen minutes earlier, hoping the drug would help settle his stomach. It seemed worse. Maybe he should smoke some more. The tall, slender, middle aged man got out of the stuffed chair and went on reconnaissance for the pot. Where had he put the stuff? Did he need to go to the bathroom again? Really, again? Yes.

Off he went down the hall to the washroom. He hated the word toilet. As a child, the other kids would chant. "T'elliot is in the toilet, T'elliot is in the toilet." They were the kind of performance poets who only worked in an oral tradition. Elliot's preference for the term throne was a recent addition to his vocabulary.

Using the word throne was a tip of the hat to the five steps to improving self confidence. It was an example of step number three. Be positive. Elliot now tried to remember what the other four steps were. Two was, don't wallow and step four was do something that indicates accomplishment. He smiled, step five was fake it. Step one he couldn't remember.

Elliot when back to the kitchen and looked out the window. It was only 4:30 in the afternoon and it was dark again. Effortlessly he abandoned step three. It wouldn't be light till something like 8:30 tomorrow morning. Then he violated step two. Eight hours of light and fourteen hours of night. Eight and fourteen, that was, a twenty-two hour day. No that wasn't right. It was sixteen hours. Sixteen hours of darkness. Christ.

It was raining with gusto too. Elliot stood, opened the cupboard, found a cookie, and devoured it. He liked the rain. It muted the city sounds and there were many of them. When it rained really hard, water gathered on the flat roofs on the buildings next to his. The roof's shallow ponds soon looked like calm lakes with raindrops peppering then. It was kind of like living at a cottage. He remembered Raisha saying. "Don't worry 'bout the rainy season, just have sex with me and listen to the raindrops till the sun comes out again." Yeah, right.

"Don't think about that, man," he said.

He watched the drops make their circular ripples and soon the rain began to ease. The sound of a traffic helicopter passing high above and occasional metal grinding from the machine shop wandered through his consciousness unnoticed. Elliot lay on his narrow bed and turned off the reading light. He closed his eyes. That's when the compressor at the skating rink started up. For a while he could ignore it but it always evolved into some other evil thing. There were four distinct sounds each with a unique range of pitch. The ra-tat-tat-tat was relentlessly consistent. The wirrwongwing came and went. The eeeeehh was faint and rose into such a high note that humans could not consciously hear it. The ahh-uh-uh-ahh was reminiscent of a gas engine failing to start.

Eliot wondered if the skating compressor was a CSIS plot to disorient the the pinko, bike riding bohemians that called his neighbourhood home. He was sure he heard a subliminal message; "the war on the car is over, the war on the car is over, the war on the car is over". He pulled a pillow over his ears as a discomforting image came in his mind. Dark figures with long curved knifes were thrust repeatedly into his torso. Each time a knife was pulled a shaft of light came shining out through the open wound.

With a groan he sat up, found his industrial ear protectors and put them on. His tension lessened instantly. Eliot was taking stock as he slouched forward, elbows on his knees, head hanging down. His sinuses were congested yet again, his gut felt like hell, even his teeth ached. He hadn't slept well for a few weeks and had taken on the habit of napping in the afternoon.

"Okay."

He lay down and found a position where he could breathe and slipped into a fretted sleep. Vivid images of gaudy coloured showgirls paraded in a desolate cityscape of crumbling architecture and wounded and suffering soldiers. Then abruptly he was a boy skating, chasing a puck with his hockey stick into a cluster of tall cattails that grew at one end of a frozen pond.

"I can't find...," he called out.

"There it is. Right there," one of the other boys pointed.

He saw the puck and stick handled it out to the open ice.

"Pass it to me Ellie. Pass it to me."

Elliot opened one eye and rolled over on his back. The curtain was drawn on the lower half of the window but through the upper half he could see the night sky. The clouds had blown away leaving a clear view of stars. A square shaft of moonlight illuminated the floor and a wooden chair near the bed.

He sat up startled. There was a boy sitting in the chair bathed in the moonlight. Elliot could see the lad wore skates.

"Hey Ellie, it's Roger. I wanted to remind you of the first step for improving self-confidence; "reconnect with old friends.'"

"Wha. How? Ah."

"Gee, Ellie, didn't mean to scare you. I just thought, you know, remember when we played on the pond behind St Teresa's and at night when the moon was full like this; and we'd play just by the light of moon."

The boy turned his face to the window and Elliot saw his features clearly.

"Roger?"

"Remember how quiet it was."

Elliot took off his hearing protectors.

"Quiet, yes."

"I guess you didn't hear I died last week. Cancer. I thought maybe your brother would have told you. He was at the funeral. It was up in Annapolis. I guess you were never at my place over in Shady Harbour. Just a sign post along the Fundy shore. Thought maybe you might have been there. They got this old time country music festival there. It's quite a draw for people. There's the fisherman's wharf too. My boat's there, pretty good wharf too really, just, you know, kinda' small. Yeah. I had a choice of what I wanted in the afterlife. Remembered playing for the altar boys hockey team. That was a happy time. Like the skates?"

Elliot looked at the skates on Rogers feet. He had no other hockey gear except the gloves and a stick that lay under the chair. He wore dark corduroy pants and a thick red sweater.

"Roger, you, didn't you..."

Elliot turned on the reading lamp. There was nothing but an empty chair beside his bed. He sat still for a long minute before hearing the sound of the ice rink compressor start up.

"Why is CSIS doing that? Are they trying to drive me crazy?"

He put on the hearing protectors and turned off the light but Roger did not reappear. Elliot stood, he was hungry but after looking into the fridge he lost his appetite. He saw himself in the entrance door mirror half way into a boxer's stance. Elliot completed it and thru a few jabs, then bobbed, weaved and danced. Uppercut, left hook, combo, jab, jab, jab. He smiled. There was still some life in the old timer.

The enemy couldn't hold up to his tenacity, and the movement was refreshing. With all his jumping and dogging, Elliot noticed a flicker of light as the tin foil covered bloom of marijuana bounced from his breast pocket to the floor. It was an brighter version of the exercise induced flashes his retinal corpuscles projection on his optic nerve. He stopped a little dizzy.

"Woo."

He did a losing your balance dance as his right foot stepped on the liberated tinfoil bundle. The crinkled surface made a Velcro-like connection to the bottom of his thick wool socks. He measured his fitness in the mirror. The socks his sister had made for him looked better than he did. Power and stamina

felt in short supply, although the shadow boxing also invigo-
rated him. Elliot grabbed his kit and made the short walk to
the gym.

*   *   *

Jorge walked in his bathing suit from the shower into the
changing room. He was a remarkably trim and fit, 75 year old
man with white hair and goatee. At the locker he removed his
bathing suit and towel-dried, then put on his gold wire frame
glasses. His mind was elsewhere as he reviewed the events of
the early afternoon. Jorge had accompanied his wife to the
doctor and while she was having some test done, he'd gone to
the library. There was a table near the library entrance that had
books the had been taken out of circulation and were for sale
at 50 cents per book. Browsing through the books, he came
across a familiar title. It was one of his books.

The moment was the definition of bittersweet. His book
had once won a literary award in his home country. He put on
his underwear and a shirt and tuned a casual glance toward the
other patrons. A trio of old Chinese men were in boisterous
Cantonese banter.

"You can't win if you don't buy a ticket," said Wendell.

He clacked-clacked along in short old man steps dressed
only in flip-flops. Jin Lee was drying his small round belly with
a towel that had a faded mermaid sitting on a rock within the
seaside design.

"He has more money than you can win on a lottery, don't
you know," Wendell added.

"My wife has all the money," Johnny, the object of their
remarks replied.

This caused a great chorus of laughter.

Jorge was a little curious about what they were laughing about. They were regulars at the pool. So was the tall blue eyed guy and the grumpy pallid man with the long surgery scar on both hips. The blue eyed guy tied his runners and stood. He nodded at Jorge. Jorge thought his name was Elliot.

"Hi, how are you?" said Jorge.

"Not bad, need to exercise. How about you?"

"Oh, you know, always the same."

"So long," said Elliot as he went to the weight room.

Jorge dried, put on his underwear and pants. The bench was like the bench in his story. The story in the discount bin at the Burnaby library. A young man put a coin in the locker and turned the key just like the men in the Mexican border bus station of his story. Jorge sat and pulled on socks and shoes. He noticed something shining on the floor. Jorge picked up the small tin foil package and folded it slightly open. He smiled.

"Marijuana."

Jorge's wife was napping when he got home so he quietly rolled the contents of the tinfoil into a single fat joint. Outside on the balcony, in the dark, he fired up his stoogie and had a couple big puffs, then butted it out leaving the doobie in the ashtray. He stood for some time looking at the apartment buildings across the street and the dark silhouette of the Douglas fir at the end of the block. The city in the distance was vague spots of light in the night fog. He could see the Christmas lights on the trees in a couple apartment windows as well as the decorated building cranes a number of blocks away.

Random thoughts and memories spiralled through his brain before he noticed how cold he felt. He went inside and into the bedroom and gently sat on the bed. Jorge was a little dehydrated from the workout and sauna and stood again intending to go to the kitchen.

"Where are you going?" she said in Spanish.

"Nadja, you are awake."

"Can you bring me a glass of water?"

"Ok."

He returned with two glasses of water and she sat up and drank.

"You smell like marijuana."

"Yes."

"I want you to make love to me."

Jorge stood and undressed.

"Light a candle," she said.

He did.

"I want to tell you how much I love the way you look after your body."

She held his scrotum in her hand as he stood beside the bed. She watched his cock thicken and then looked up at him.

"And I like the way you look after me," she said before she started stroking him, massaging his big balls. Jorge watched her hands move gracefully back and forth, each movement a line in a poem.

"You never fail me," she giggled.

"Nor you me."

She lay on her back and threw back the covers, spit on her fingers and rubbed them on her pussy. "I'm ready," she said.

They both chuckled as he furrowed into her.

"Ah yes, that's what Nadja needs."

"Oh, you beautiful creature."

"Husband, that feels so...oh."

The muscles in Jorge's body sang joyful and vigorous. Nadja was electric and with each thrust she whispered in pleasure. Jorge held his torso up with his arms and his hips pushed over and over and over between his wife's legs. The volcano was about to erupt, the hurricane arrive at landfall, the dam beginning to burst.

She came and the hair on Jorge's forearms stood up as if they were a singing a note worthy of a great Russian choir. She was still and he went limp and rolled off and to the side. She closed her eyes as if she was prepared to sleep. Jorge lay on his back looking at the ceiling. After a few minutes he noticed a distant sound. It was that big thing on the roof of the hockey rink. He stood and pulled a thick curtain across the bedroom window. It was silent again. Then he went to extinguish the candle. He could see the reflection of his head and shoulders in the dresser mirror. Life is so short, so fleeting, the reflection reminded him. Jorge blew out the candle.

* * *

In the early light of a sunny morning a crow landed on Jorge and Nadja's balcony railing. She was a maiden and like the majority of crows, she was likely to remain one. Only a few members of the species ever get a chance to mate because their populations far outnumber the available nesting sites. A life of celibacy for the greater good of the tribe had caused no tarnish on the grandeur of her aristocratic strut. Still she kept aware for other birds, especially seagulls.

The crow was curious about the joint in the ashtray and for a moment gave it her undivided attention. It seemed to be partly cooked although it tasted unlike anything that reminded her of food. Perhaps one of her friends could enlighten her on its purpose, so she picked it up, adjusted for its weight and flew off toward the harbour. She turned, flying over the hockey rink. What a racket, she thought. The happy crow veered east and landed a couple blocks later on the roof of the Volga River Cafe and Bakery. There were a lot of quick visits to the cafe by the off-to-work crowd. A new car arrived. Surrey white, thought the crow, what a nice colour.

It was Lorrie's car and she was checking her reflection in the car mirror. She looked younger than her twenty-seven years. Her phone rang and she recognized the number as her mother's.

"Hello, mama," she said in Cantonese.

"Where are you?" the mother replied in Mandarin. Lorrie rolled her pretty eyes at her mother's predictable contrariness. Lorrie switched to Mandarin.

"Just getting a coffee and picking up my friend and then heading to the states to do some shopping."

"Who are you going with?"

"Kiko."

"That Japanese girl."

"She's half Korean."

"She's still Japanese. Your grandfathers will be wailing in their graves."

"I'm sure my grandfathers have other things to worry about."

"Don't be disrespectful. That's what happens when you fraternize with the Japanese, you lose respect for your ancestors."

Lorrie's skin was so flush with heat she reached up and opened the sunroof. The cool air quickly crept in as her mother kept up her crazy talk.

"Ok mama, thanks for that, I'll see you when I get home, late tonight."

She hung up and went to the door that was the entrance to the apartments above the Volga River Cafe and Bakery. Kiko's voice answered the buzzer.

"Hello."

"Hi, it's me Lorrie."

"Hey, you're early. Come in."

Lorrie ran up the stairs. Her long slender arms and legs moved like they had rubber joints or like a youth who had just gone through a growing spurt and wasn't familiar with their new gangly body.

Kiko met her at the door in a loose-fitting silky housecoat. She was short and muscular, her sturdy shape enhanced by her passion for swimming and weightlifting. They embraced and kissed. On the stove the coffee came to a boil.

"Want some?" said Kiko. She adjusted her black frame glasses and went to the stove. Lorrie followed her and quickly wrapped her long arms around Kiko from behind.

"God, I missed you."

Kiko smiled as Lorrie slid her hand down her friend's flat belly and over the soft black hair of her pubic mound.. Her long fingers sought out the center of the universe. Kiko turned her head and their wet mouths came together.

"I missed you too," Kiko whispered, eagerly giving in to Lorrie's magic fingers. After a few minutes Kiko's hips humped in short vigorous thrusts and she held her weight with her hands on each side of the stove.

"Can you come standing up?" said Lorrie.

"I don't know. I think so."

Outside, on the roof the crow was growing impatient. Where were her pals so she could show them what she had found? She was starting to feel a little hungry too. The crow picked up the joint that lay on the roof between her feet and glided down to the roof of Lorrie's expensive Mazda, a Japanese car the crow knew to be named after a Persian god. The crow herself, a Mohawk mistress of law, thought her shiny black feathers a nice and elegant contrast to the Mazda's Surrey white.

She stuck her head in the open sunroof. She couldn't see any food, besides her body was to big for the opening. That's when she saw the grey seagull distorted by the concave glass of the sunroof, plunging down toward her. Shocked, the crow fled, dropping its curio onto the passenger seat which then bounced to the floor. Seeing the crow holding nothing but her charm, the seagull gave up his pursuit and gracefully surged upward toward the patches of blue that came and went beyond the quick moving clouds.

Lorrie and Kiko opened the dark green door of the Volga River smiling and went to the Mazda.

"You have your passport?" said Lorrie.

"Yes," replied Kiko, holding up her ornate Mexican leather bag.

They got in the car and Kiko put the bag on the floor on top of Jorge's finely crafted doobie. Kiko did up her seat belt and looked over at her lover.

"I'm glad you came early. Thank you for that."

Lorrie pushed up her sunglasses. "Just doing the Lord's good work, doll. Do you want to grab a sandwich before we get on the highway."

"I've been craving pizza, actually."

"Well, it is nearly lunch time," Lorrie laughed. "Megabite?"

"Absolutely."

They drove to the pizza store and parked. Lorrie read the byline on the Megabite sign.

"Pizza for the computer age. Look," Lorrie pushed her sunglasses down her short nose and looked at Kiko over them. "They're hiring."

"Maybe we could work together," Kiko laughed, grabbing her bag. Lorrie watched her go into Megabite, then reached up and closed the sunroof. She leaned back against the head rest and closed her eyes. She wondered if she should phone her mother and ask if she wanted her to pick something up for her in the states. Capri pants, that's all she ever wanted. Lorrie could buy her a pair, there was no reason to phone really. She took a deep breath. What was that smell? She opened her eyes and looked about, then she spotted it and picked it up. Christ, it was marijuana.

"Vegie supreme," Kiko said getting into the car.

"What, you got the munchies?"

"Ahh."

Lorrie held up the dope and continued. "How could, we're crossing the border, ump, bozo. What are you doing with this?"

"Tampon?"

"Marijuana, weed, pot, come on. If they stop us at the border, wow, what were you thinking? It stinks. You stink." Lorrie opened the sunroof again.

"Take it easy Lorrie. That's not mine. I don't smoke pot. It's your car."

"It came from your Latino smugglers backpack there. It was right there."

"I don't know how it... That is not mine."

"So it just fell from the sky, did it?" said Lorrie.

Kiko took the joint, rolled down her window and tossed it to the sidewalk. "There, it's gone. Shall we proceed."

There was a clunk on the roof of the car. A crow was looking in through the open sunroof. They both looked up.

"Craw, craw."

They looked at each other, then Lorrie turned on the engine. "I'm getting my mother Capri pants."

"What colour?"

"Lime green."

"How about hot pink?"

"No, she has a hot pink pair already," she laughed.

As she put the car into traffic, a stooped man in shabby clothes came up the sidewalk, surveying the concrete for cigarette butts. He bent down, rescued another candidate, broke off the filter and placed the paper-wrapped tobacco in a small, foul smelling, transparent bag. His radar spotted the discarded joint from a distance.

"Gees, a millionaire," he said picking up the fat stogy and immediately recognized the uniqueness of his latest discovery. "Cool, weed. To the victor go the spoils."

The victor went to the end of the block and then down the alley behind Megabite Pizza. There between two dumpsters he took a closer look at his find and searched his pockets for a lighter. A head popped up from the open dumpster.

"Hey Victor, are you divin'?"

"Victor don't dive."

"Well, excuse me."

"Victor don't wanta' put you in the poorhouse. You should be grateful."

"I should be a lot of things. You got a cigarette, Victor? "

"I got some street blend."

Diver looked at the plastic bag of butts Victor presented.

"Street blend," said Diver and he rolled a cigarette.

"You look like you've been swallowed by a whale in that dumpster. Any good finds."

"Book on D-I-O-G-E-N-I-S. There's a picture. He lived in a barrel."

"Never heard of him."

"Me neither."

"I got some weed, Wanta' smoke some?"

"No, It screws up my medication."

Victor laughed. "Yeah. I get my shot at the end of the month."

"A shot."

"Amilldamnillmorofien."

"Never heard of it."

"And this if I can get it."

Victor held up the joint and lit it as Diver got out of the dumpster.

"See you at the Kettle then. Nearly feeding time."

Victor didn't respond and Driver hiked the bag of empty cans on his bike and pedalled away. Victor turned the joint into smoke and ash. He wasn't prepared for the strength of the drug. He watched a crow land on the roof of the cinder block building across the alley. It was a mechanical crow, he could tell by the way it marched back and forth, back and forth. It had been sent to make sure he wouldn't escape. Victor paced between the dumpsters, his heart pumping quickly.

"What are you going to do, huh, what?" he said.

"It wasn't my fault, you brought me here," Victor answered his own question

"Sure that's what everybody says."

"Everybody, who's everybody?"

"It's a secret. Don't you know anything."

"Everything a secret, isn't that right."

"I'll tell you okay, but don't tell anybody. It's the batteries. They don't last very long. I'll have to fly back to headquarters and get new batteries soon. Just watch, but don't make it obvious. Hear that sound? It sounds like the dry cleaner place. That's their signal. They're saying you better come back soon and get new batteries."

"Is that where the headquarters is? The dry cleaning place?"

"No, no, man. The signal comes from the hockey rink and that signal comes from the cold storage place."

"What cold storage place?"

"The Chinese cold storage place across the parking lot from the hockey rink. The big concrete place with no windows. That's the headquarters. They keep their information in there and the batteries for the robot crows. You never see anybody come in and out of that place. CSIS comes and goes through a tunnel underground."

"Tunnel, where does that lead?"

"I don't know, but we should try to find out, don't you think?"

"Yeah."

"Shhh, somebody's coming."

One of the young handsome Turks who worked at Megabite came out of the store's alley exit. He wore a plaid cap with ear flaps and carried a full pizza bag. Alper was off on a delivery. He saw Victor and smiled.

"Hello sir, how are you?"

Victor only grunted and rolled his weight from one foot to the other, but the contact broke his psychotic episode and as the pizza man sped off, so did the crow. Victor wandered back down the alley to the sidewalk. He felt hungry. The school kids were already flooding in for the lunch special. Two slices and a pop for five dollars.

Francesca and her sister were quickly serving up the slices and keeping the shelf supplied with fresh pizza out of the oven.

"Another Hawaiian. Put in a Pepperoni too, okay," Francesca said in Tagalog.

Victor watched through the large plate glass window. He rooted through his pockets, 35 cents. Hum, 4.65 short. He could get a free healthy lunch at the Kettle, hang out with those crazies, but he had his heart set on the pizza special.

Victor divided what he needed by 2, That was 2.325. Then he took the square root of that. That calculation needed the help of the cod fish look. He rolled his eyes up so only the whites were showing.

"One point five, two, four, ah, seven. Umm."

Victor looked up and down the sidewalk. He was indeed hungry for pizza. He wanted pizza. He needed pizza. Could he panhandle. Not the kids. He had some pride after all. Victor saw a man needing a shave in expensive shoes.

"Elliot, hey, Elliot. How are you today?"

Elliot was surprised the homeless looking guy knew his name.

"Ah, fine, thanks," he said, not breaking his stride. Victor followed him.

"Hey, Elliot could you buy me the pizza special?"

Elliot stopped and turned around.

"Two slices and a pop." Victor said pointing at the lunch special sign. Elliot weighed the request.

"No," he said and turned back into his world.

"Elliot, wait, remember me, I'm Roger."

Elliot stopped and turned a second time. "Roger?"

"Yeah, we used to play hockey together, remember, for the altar boys. I got thirty-five cents. I need four, sixty-five. Half of that is two dollars and thirty-two cents and the square root of that is one, point five, two, four, seven, nine, five."

"Alright, alright, alright."

They got in line with the chatty students. When they got to the counter Francesca said, "Hello, Elliot. Are you buying the lunch special for your friend again?"

"Yes. What do you want Roger?"

"Ohh, I'd like the bacon crumble and, ah, the feta, spinach and an ice tea, please."

"Anything for you Elliot?" Francesca smiled.

"No, no, I already ate at the Kettle. I'm full."

"Ok. Here's your pizza Victor. Bye."

The men stepped outside.

"Gee, that pop cooler in there is really loud. It must drive them crazy," said Victor.

"Yeah," said Elliot. "It must."

Paris of the Pacific Northwest

Celeste was an athletic women in her early fifties. The gymnastics and competitive wrestling of her youth had defined her physique and her passion for weight training maintained it. She wandered about her apartment in white underwear while listening to her cell phone. She examined a number of skirts and dresses hanging in the closet, then passed through the living room. There she played a C chord on a small electric piano. Then the actor went into the kitchen. She sighed, looking disdainfully at the plates submerged in cold water in the sink. Celeste placed one hand on her hip as she spoke.

"No, I told them I can't do that, I can't, I won't… It's supposed to be funny? It's not… Nooo, childbirth, a dog. Once was enough for that guy… A women giving birth to a dog, just isn't funny…No,…Well that's what I told them. It's not TV… No, it's a movie and really, the money wasn't even that good, honestly."

Celeste stood on her toes, stretched and rolled her head. She looked as if she hear the crack, crack of her neck, then she strolled back to the clothes closet.

"I can't think of anyone either, maybe someone young, you know, really young. Anyway, today I have an audition... oh thanks, it's this afternoon. And get this, I'm being raped... No, raped and, well, I'm trying to pick out an outfit right now... Oh, of course, that's okay. Why don't I call you later... Okay, thanks, bye."

Celeste picked out a small skirt and wiggled it on. She cut an attractive figure in the mirror on the closet door, enough to inspire a bit of comic song and dance.

"Down by the bay, where the water melons grow,

Back to my home, I dare not go,

For if I do, my mother will say,

Did you ever see an iguana, smoking marijuana?

Down by the bay."

Jason entered, drink in hand and sat at the piano. He plunked out the melody notes to her last two lines.

"Hi."

"Hey," he replied and played a dark chord.

"What's up?"

"Nothin'."

"How does this look?"

"Not old enough," he said and played a cheery riff.

"Who, you or me?" she asked sarcastically.

"Is that yours or mine?" he asked, ignoring her tone and pointing at her head.

"You have a grey wig?"

"Yeah."

"Really! Well, I'll be..."

"There's lot's about me you don't know."

"Apparently," Celeste tossed the grey wig on a chair and fitted on a red one, "Well, this one's mine. I wore it in Paris of the Pacific Northwest, oh, nearly eight years ago."

"I hate that fake Steamboat Gothic style."

"Hate. Now that's a strong reaction. You like musicals, Jason."

She looked at him, waiting for a response. He stared solemnly at his hands. Celeste shrugged turning back toward the mirror, "You're in a funny mood," she said, taking off her pale blue shirt.

Jason stood and and watched her reflection as she buttoned up an elegant satin blouse.

"What do you think of this one?" she said.

He didn't reply, just turned away and sat down again at the piano. Celeste moved closer to the mirror, examining her face. "Eight years, oh my," she said to herself and then spoke louder for Jason's benefit, "I really enjoyed that show. I had a great song. It was so much fun, and the cast...wonderful. And there was this Filipino dancer, God, he was hung like a horse. Ha, and there was also this black American kid. His looked like a cashew. Funny isn't it. Just the opposite of the stereotype. But, Alfonso, oh, Alfonso, he wa..."

"I've heard this before," Jason interrupted and played three discordant chords, "Do you know your lines?" he asked with a discontented tone.

"My lines? Well, the last one: 'No, stop, no, ahhh.'"

Jason refused to smile but played and sang part of a song.

"At night we sit in those hip cafes, No one seems to care who pays,

And all we do seems A-OK, cause pretty soon, someone bound to say,

Out here on the west coast, we know we are blessed,

Here in the Paris of the Pacific Northwest."

"That's it. That was my song," Celeste laughed. "To bad you never saw it."

"Don't you want to run your lines?" he asked again.

"Oh, that's so sweet, honey. The script is there on the kitchen table. I don't like these shoes. They're, I don't know..."

"This thing. Is this the script"? he said abrasively.

"What's that you're drinking?" she asked looking away from the mirror.

"The last of the scotch in the, ah, cabinet. Why?"

"That's expensive, you know."

"Well, it all tastes the same to me."

"That was your mother's, Jason. A gift from an ardent admirer."

"She'll forgive me, if she finds out. You don't have to tell her." he said innocently. He spoke aggressively again, "It says here you're supposed to be sixty. The shoes are fine, for God's sake. What a fuss budget."

He sat and placed this elbows on the keyboard and rested his chin on his hands.

"Okay, okay, you want sixty, throw me the damn grey wig... There, sexy sixty. The aging trophy bride. I could play this character in my sleep, but still I have too. After all, somebody's got to work around here."

"Once upon a time trophy bride," he laughed. "So who's the philandering husband? How many scenes are you in?"

"Not enough. I get two days tops," she answered exasperated, still finger combing the wig.

"Who's the husband?" Jason yelled.

"You shouldn't drink in the middle of the day. You know what I mean. I don't want you to frighten me, understand."

"Sorry, but seriously, who's the stud pony?" His cheeks had turned deep pink.

"I need to learn how to pronounce it. It's like eight syllables long. He's had a long and successful career in Bollywood films. His nick name, Ram," she said, trying to remain calm.

"Appropriate."

"The casting director said he's has remarkable charm. It may do you a good to met him."

"Do you know about bonobos monkeys?" Jason changed the subject.

"Is that a Cirque du Soleil show?" Celeste said, self absorbed, changing her shoes.

"Yes," said Jason and finished his drink.

"I'd like to see one of their shows. Too bad they're so damn expensive."

"The only taboo bonobos have is sex between mother and son, every other sexual encounter is acceptable, encouraged."

"Encouraged," Celeste did a little spin. "What do you think?"

"Your character doesn't have a name," said Jason looking at the script.

"No, just Ex-wife, I think."

"Rapist, doesn't have a name either. So what's this Ram dude do, anyway."

"He feels guilt and seeks vengeance. No name rapist, no name ex-wife, welcome to the movies. Now, this scene, I haven't done something quite like this before. So, I want to nail this. We need the money."

"That's for sure."

"I come in like this and seeing you startles me so I go into the corner."

"I've been watching you, following you," Jason reads.

"How did,....Wait I need my handbag. I might be able to do some business with it. Okay, I love that voice Jason, very creepy. Alright, go ahead."

"I've been watching you, following you."

"How did, how did you get in here?"

"The front door," he laughed. "Sorry, really the front door? Who writes this stuff?"

"You're not being very helpful Jason. Back door, front door, barn door, I don't care."

"Alright, alright, alright... I've been watching you, following you."

"How did, how did you get in here?"

"The front door," he said deviously.

"You shouldn't be here. This is a private residence."

"Oh my."

"Please, just go, just leave now."

"Shut up."

"Please, look, take the money, look, please...take, take it...."

"I don't want your stinking money. Just come here. Feel this."

"No! Stop! No! Ahhhh."

Jason put the script on the piano. He slowly removed her wig and griped a fist full of Celeste's auburn hair.

"That's it Jason, stop! You're hurting me. Jason, it's not funny, stop fooling around, watch my clothes. Stop it. Cut it out."

"Shut up."

Jason pushed her to the floor and held her by the neck as he sat on top of her.

"What the hell is wrong with you? Look I've got to get ready, my audition," she said chocking.

"Fuck you."

"I can't breathe. Jason, please."

"You're so precious, so special. I'll show you something special."

"You're hurting me. Please, please stop."

Jason slid his hand under her dress, then undid his belt.

"You like that?" he said before Celeste began striking him with her thrashing fists. He leaned back trying to avoid her bodybuilder punches. It was enough for her to free herself from under his tall, slim frame and get to her feet.

"Stop it, Jason. You're scaring me. Please don't," she pleaded backing toward the kitchen sink. Celeste's hand went into the cold water and she felt the bone handle of a knife.

"The rapist has a name now. What is it? What's my name?" he raged.

She swung the knife in front of her. Wildly, Jason lunged toward her, his large, bony hands grasping for her forearms. Together they fell to the floor with a thud. Jason's face was direct above hers, mouth agape, distorted like a Haida wood demon mask. His weight had forced the sharp blade to pierce deeply into his abdomen. He gasped with a griming sound and reared upright to his knees. His trembling hands cupped the dark blood streaming out around the intact knife. Celeste watched in a frozen moment.

"Oh my god, oh my god, oh Jason, Jason," Celeste spoke in a hollow voice. She entered 911 into her phone. "Hello, hello. I need someone. Help, I need help. My son, he's hurt. Hello, yes, Celeste, yes, 520 Glen Street...Okay," she said and put the phone down as the faint voice of the dispatcher droned on. Celeste watched Jason tumbled to the side. His head struck the keys of the piano, before falling face-first to the floor in front of her.

There was the sound of one person slowly clapping. Celeste stood and walked forward to the front of the stage. Her clear voice carried effortlessly over the empty rows of crimson red seats to the darkest place at the back of the theatre. "How was that? Do you want to run it again or break for lunch?"

"Lucia, you were great as always my dear, just great. And the blood, that was fantastic. Works beautifully. I'd like to run it again and then go for lunch. You okay Mike?" the director said.

"Sure, but you know, I really like the original Grand Guignol script where she cuts my dick off," he said, grinning.

"Mike, that's not going to happen. That was Paris in 1918. This is Vancouver, 2018, you know, we just can't risk it. The audience might go for it but...Besides, staging that is pretty damn tricky."

"I've known men who have volunteered for the process, my dear. Last thing we need is some strange interpretation from the trans rights mob, trying to shut the show down," added Lucia.

"Really!" said Mike.

"Well, maybe, I don't know," she said, making a goofy face.

"Okay, okay, you guys, we're all getting hungry here. Let's run the scene one more time, and no need for the blood sack this time, Mike."

"Fair enough."

Jason went backstage and Celeste put the props back in place after drying her hands. She held the cell phone to her ear and appeared to be listening as she went from the closet to the kitchen and then back to the closet. She placed her free hand on her hip and spoke.

"No, I can't do that, I can't, I won't… It's supposed to be funny? It's not... Nooo, childbirth, a dog. Once was enough for that guy... A woman, giving birth to a dog, just isn't funny... No...Well that's what I told them. It's not even TV, it's a movie, who knows, the money wasn't that good either... I can't think of anyone who..., Maybe someone young, you know, really young. Today I have an audition...oh thanks, it's this afternoon. And get this. I'm being raped... No, raped and, well, I'm trying to pick out an outfit right now...

Nancy of the Pizza Garden

<u>a short play</u>
by
Kempton Dexter

First performed in the Havana Theatre
during the Vancouver Fringe Festival
2012

Actors

T.T.- Roxy Hamilton

Travis – Richard Newman

Alex – Micheal Kopsa

Music by Hi-rise Dex

Directed by Anthony Ingram

Artist studio with a number of paintings on the floor, leaning as if against the walls. Small table and chairs. At the easel, Travis is painting. Alex, the art dealer, is standing holding a painting. (director's note: paintings are empty frames.) Music theme, Girl trouble, which is also Alex's cellphone ring.

A   I like the landscapes Travis, but I remember you used to do a lot of figure work.

T   Well, most of the new paintings are here. There's figures in the landscapes. *(begins to clean up)*

A   Oh yeah. I see that.

T   I like this one here. *(the painting he's working on)* It has a story. *(cleans brushes)*

A   Um hum. Stories are good.

T   It's an abandoned copper mine near Golden. It's kinda grown over now. But back in the early 1900's there was a big strike there. Government sent in a bunch of goons and kicked the families out of their houses and busted a lot of heads.

A   Okay.

T   Now, there's just a dim hole in the mountain and everything is covered over with bush and trees and stuff. Forgotten like we forget our past, our history.

A   Right, hum, no figures.

T   No, I thought about putting a old guy on a horse. But.

A   Old guy on a horse. Well, I like horses. Hey this one's good.

T   Cute chick.

A   Yeah, She's a long ways away. Nice composition. Is there some symbolism here?

T   No, I was just into the clouds mostly.

A   She is a cute chick. You used to paint some seriously erotic work. Got to say man, I loved that stuff. I tell ya buddy, sex never goes out of fashion.

T   Yeah. *(pause)* Do you want a beer, coffee? I've got some Glen-something or other.

A   Scotch?

T   Yep.

A   Glen-something or other. Please and thank you lad.

T   *(goes upstage, out of light)* You're on the rocks, right?

A   Still, yep. The work's...solid. The labour history? You wanta lead an exhibit with something, ah, you know, boom. Yeah. With a...

T   Glen Ord. That's it.*(returns)* Rosie brought it back from Scotland. She was there earlier this year. Muir-of-Ord. That's the village they distill this. Now, all my daughters have visited their granny's homeland. Slange-ah-vah.

A   Glen Ord. Hum.

T   It's booze.

A   Not bad. What else is here? Let's see. Okay! Wow, Travis. I like this. Wow man. Now that's a good painting. You son of a gun. You been holding out on me man. Geez.

T   That one?

A   Yeah, it's really raw. It's great. *(takes a big drink, shudders)* Woo. Who is this?

T   Ah, that's Nancy.

A   Nancy, strong, immediate, nice youthful energy. Good work, Travis, beautiful man .

T.   Well, it's a real old painting of mine, Alex. A real old one.

A   I've never seen it before. How old?

T   Ah, like nearly forty years ago.

A   Really. Interesting, interesting.

T   Yeah, a buddy, Jack bought it way back and, well, he died last year, and his wife didn't want it around, you know, so she just gave it back to me, wanted me to have it, you know, yeah and she said, she said, it was haunted.

A   Haunted? Really. Could be a good marketing angle. You want to sell this?

T   Sure.

A   You were pretty young then, early twenties, I guess. I like this one. I mean, I love your new stuff, you know. She was a girlfriend, right?

T   No, she stayed in my studio for a while. Slept there. That's the bed she's sitting on. I can't remember how long, three or four months maybe.

A   Really. Hum. If you look carefully you can tell this is by the same guy who's still finding his style. Nice. The same guy who has done these mature works.

T   Well it is and it isn't the same guy. Still the same stupid guy doing stupid jobs to get by.

A   Hey man, it's just ah, rough patch. Let's hope we sell a shit load of these paintings. They're good enough. Sweet.

T   Well you know, it's been fifteen years since I've had an art show. I'm flattered you want to show me. Honestly.

A   Hey, you deserve it man.

T   Thanks Alex. You're right about this painting. It's loaded. Freaked me out when I got it. You know what I mean.

A   She looks troubled, dangerous, and well, sexy. You must have got down hot and heavy with her.

T   No, no man. I was married then. You remember Sunny. Hell man, she was a full time job in the sack, man. There was no messin' around.

A   Well, that's not what I heard.

T   That was later.

A   So how did you meet this, Nancy?

T   Well, it was, ah, at the pizzeria.

A   She worked there?

T   No, I did. I was the delivery guy. And Sunny and I, we had this great apartment, the top floor of an old farm house on the edge of town. It was a kilometre or so from work and I could take the delivery van home most nights. Anyway, it was closing time and she'd been hanging around there for a couple hours. She said her mother had kicked her out. That's it. Had no place to go.

A   Kicked her out. How old was she?

T   Geez, fifteen or sixteen, almost sixteen I think.

A   Fifteen, oh, oh.

T   Anyway, seems to me if I can remember right, she wanted to stay in the pizza place. I said something like, ah, 'Imagine the owner opening in the morning and finding a teenage girl inside'. She, well, she said something about phoning a teacher who would help her out but there was no answer. She had no place to go. So what could I do. I offered to let her sleep in the studio room in the apartment. There was a little cot in there.

A   Oh yeah, I see. So how did your wife like that?

T   Oh, she wasn't all that hip to the idea. It was after 2 am but she was in bed still awake, I remember. But, you know it was January on the east coast. Couldn't just leave the kid on the street.

A   No, I suppose not.

T   Anyway, after a couple days I get hold of the teacher guy and he says she ran away. So Sunday night, I think it was, the mother, er, the foster mother shows up and takes the kid home. The mother was a pretty severe piece of work too. Nancy had painted a vivid image of the old gal. So like, Mr. Dumb nice guy, I tell the kid if it really is that bad, when she turns sixteen she can come live with us for a while and get a job or something. A month later she moves in.

A   She had charm and disarm pal. Ha. Charm and disarm.

T   I suppose. It all went bad pretty fast. She stole stuff and lied and my drunk bohemian artist pals wanted to get into her pants. And Sunny wasn't happy at all.

A   No, I bet. Sunny, I liked her.

T   Can't blame her I guess. She never said I told you so. I did that all by myself.

A   Teenage anguish, anger, angst. It's there alright. There's more too. Geez, it's a hell of a painting, Travis.

T   Yeah.

A   So, Sunny kicked her out?

T   No, oh no. Nancy left on her own. It was obvious she wasn't welcome. After a while, we heard she ended up in Halifax.

A   It's hard to help people. They can take, well, you can throw good money after bad. It's tough to know when to stop.

T   Well, I remember a year or so later, I was on a city bus in Halifax, somewhere in the north end, can be rough there. From the bus window, I saw this overweight girl sitting on the front step of ah, old run down house. With a baby on her lap. It was her for sure. That same expression.

Those eyes. Those eyes man. Hum. Maybe I should make a painting of that.

A   So much for her search for independence.

T   Yeah. How's your drink. Another?

A   Well, I... *(cell phone rings)* Hello, hello, ah, hello..., it's dead.

T   The reception's kinda funny here. Stand by the window. *(rings again)*

A   Hello. Oh hey baby, how's it going... Must be my tinfoil hat... No, I'm still here...ah, we just got started really... No...Well, ah, come over? I guess. *(Travis nods yes)* OK sure. Ah, it's 3290 Dumfries... Dumb fries, stupid chips. That's right, buzzer number 2. Yeah. Okay. Sure... No, just Travis... no problemento. Okay. 3290, number 2... Right... Okay. Okay, yeah... Okay, bye, yeah, bye. Geez.

T   What's up?

A   Oh nothing, just Cindy, likes to track me down, you know, where were you, who were you with, when will you be home?

T   Short leash.

A   Sometimes I feel like I'm dating CSIS. When she's happy it's great. Never lasts that long. Worst thing is she doesn't trust me.

T   Well, you are an art dealer, after all. *(toasts)*

A   She can be so sweet, you know, but, she doesn't want me spending time alone with my women friends. I have to ask her permission. She says, "Why can't you be more like Travis?"

T   Me, what, she wants to date a monk?

A   I tell her Travis is a big dog too, used to be. I tell her, "Since I met you there's no messing around with other women." *(phone rings)* I better answer it. Hey baby... Hello. Yeah the reception's bad... Hum, I don't know, I'll see. Travis, you want to go out for sushi? Travis says no. You sure Travis? It will be our treat. He had some at lunch. He's not... Some other time. Uh, sure, okay. See you soon. Okay, bye.

T   Thanks, but no, I've got an idea for this painting I want to work on tonight. I better stay around the studio, I could finish it tonight.

A   Oh, another landscape?

T   Maybe, maybe even do her again. What do you think?

A   Of what you think she looks like now?

T   I never thought of that, that's interesting. No, not what she might look like now. Just memory. I've been thinking a lot about those times lately. I guess that's where I'm getting my mojo. There's a certain self indulgence to it. If I was a knife thrower in the circus, I'd have certainly killed a lot of assistants over the years. I always thought being self critical drove me to a higher level. Maybe it just makes you wanta hide. You know that song, ah. *sings,* It don't come easy. You know it don't come easy. Dumpie, dumpie, da, da dumpie dumpie da, you know it come easy. You know that one. Ringo did it.

A   Ah, doesn't sound all that familiar.

T   Gee man, it sure looks easy for some of those cats, know what I mean. What's up, Alex?

A   Ah, it's Cindy. Driving me crazy.

T   What?

A   Text. Do you want to order pizza?

T   Pizza. Hell yeah. Haven't had pizza in a long time. Pepperoni, mushrooms, green pepper or...

A   Okay. She's got some place she likes. Sure, sorry.

T   No worries. How about this one?

A   Ah, just a second. There. Ah, this one? Where this, er ah, who's this?

T   That's Chief Paul, and that's the band's fishing boat there. That's ah, Deep Bay and this is a, ass-hole retired banker guy.

A   This is new?

T   Oh yeah.

A   Weird.

T   What daya mean?

A   Oh, this over here in the painting. Looks like freaky wood carving at the entrance of the driveway. Kind of native, West coast.

T   Oh that, yes, banker dude, no, accountant, corporate tax accountant. He'd been a big cheese with Mac-Blo.

A   The thing is huge.

T   Yeah, it is. Dude's job was to figure out ways of not paying taxes.

A   That's handy.

T   Dude was very proud of that sculpture. He said he bought it on the dock in Prince Rupert. Drunk Indian guy wanted ten dollars for it. Banker paid five. He was very pleased with the deal, very pleased with himself about that. I did quite a bit of landscaping for that guy. Man the bastard was cheap.

A   So there's a story to this one too.

T   How's your drink?

A   Geez, I got a bit of a buzz off this stuff, man.

T   Well, we're having pizza. How about a beer or wine?

A   Wine, good idea.

T   Right on. *(from side or offstage)* I got some Californian red here.

A   Californian? I thought you were an Okanagan man.

T   Christ, I drink anything. Rosie left it. Since the Americans invaded Iraq, she buys Yankee vino.

A   Why is that?

T   Her protest.

A   Protest?

T   Make wine, not war. *(returns)* Cheers.

A   Up the queen.

T   Ha, ha. Right you are Caper. Up the queen.

A   Long live Cape Breton.

T   Hey, hey. Cape Breton always. Geez, good to see you again Ali.

A   Like wise. Good to know Rosie keeps an eye on you. She's a great kid. You're a lucky man Travis.

T   Yeah, yeah. Raised a good kid. Guess, I did something right. So Alex, do you think anything will sell?

A   Sure, why not.

T   Cuz it's art and cuz it's shit.

A   Well, you'd be surprised at what people buy.

T   That's reassuring.

A   Selling it. That's my job, buddy.

T   Hey man, Davey was here last week.

A   Ah, Deep Dave or Deal in the Ditch Dave?

T   Deal in the Ditch.

A   Geez. So how was that? What's he doing?

T   He's selling real estate.

A   Seriously?

T   Yeah. I have his card here somewhere, but he brought a gift. Check it out.

A   Woo, woo, woo. Hashish. Deal in the Ditch Dave.

T   Smell good, hah. Want a pipe? Hot knives?

A   Geez man, you're the same old Travis. Man, what a glorious bouquet. Oh, *(cell)* It's Cindy. Hello beautiful... What...What the, what were... Oh for... That's my, my private account Cindy. Geez. You've got no right. Hello, hello. Christ.

T   Is she coming over?

A   No, no man. She's been checking my phone calls, the records. I hate that.

T   Some gal's number?

A   Any gal. Gees, she's ah, ah, a fucking detective. Thing is I'm being good... Where's that pipe?

T   Here, fire it up. Wow, I didn't know she was so jealous.

A   That's not the half of it.

T   I'm sorry to hear you guys are having, ah, trouble. Should I phone her? Ask her to come over?

A   No, Just give it some air.

T   Okay. So, how's the pipe man?

A   Good, good. Here.

T   Umm. Burnin good.

A   So Deal in the Ditch Dave living in town now.

T   No, Alberta, Calgary.

A   Selling real estate. God. You know I bet that painting would sell right away. Trouble is, it's worth more than we could ask for it right now. Not many know your work anymore.

T   They never did.

A   Hey man, that's not true. There was interest. You should have hung in there man.

T   Yeah.

A   So, she claimed it was haunted. Wow. And you never had sex with her?

T   No, absolutely not, too young, man. I'm pretty sure Jack did. He was around at the time. He'd never admit to it. He was like that you know. Very private about his fire hose action.

A   Jack's wife knew I bet. That's why she gave the painting back. That's what's haunting her.

T   Maybe. She said the eyes followed her around the room.

A   Eyes followed her around.

T   The painting. Nancy's eyes followed her around. Thing is Nancy jumped off the John A. MacDonald.

A   The bridge to Dartmouth?

T   Yeah. After that they said the painting was haunted.

A   She died.

T   Oh yeah. *(doorbell)*

A   Jumpin' Christ man, what was that?

T   It's the doorbell. Hello.

TT   Pizza Garden.

T   Pizza Garden. Come on in. She ordered a pizza. That was fast. Let's hope it was before she snooped your records.

A   Pizza man, gees. I'm not hungry.

T   You will be. Come on in. *(enter pizza delivery person)*

TT   Hi guys. $25. 23

T $25.23. Sure.

A   Hey, hey. Let me get that. Hi. Here's $30, Okay.

TT   Thanks, man.

T   Hey dude, you like a draw?

TT   Draw?

A   You know, a toke.

TT   Ha, Sure, why not. Okay.... Wow, tasty.

A   Busy sweetheart?.

TT   Oh yeah, game night.

A   Game?

TT   Canucks and Winnipeg, tied, middle of the third.

T   Winnipeg, right on.

A   You're a hockey fan, how about that.

TT   Yeah, I listen on the car radio. In bit and pieces, you know.

A   You don't see a pizza delivery chick, er I mean...

T.T.   No worries. There's a few of us out there. I used to deliver pizza in Yellowknife. Tips were really good there.

T   Yellowknife. Gee, that's, well? Here's to great tips. How do they say cheers in Yellowknife?

TT   Fuckin ahy.

T/A Fuckin' ahy. *(laughter)*

A   Right on.

TT   Hey, wow, that's Nancy, wow, cool. You have Nancy. How...

A   You know this painting?

TT   Sure. I made that painting.

A   You, you. You made this painting?

TT   Yep. That's my painting alright. Look at the back. Nancy from the Pizza Garden and my stamp, TT

A   Hum. That's right TT.

TT   Teresa Trembley. That's me. Someone bought it for $50 from a group show, a benefit for the homeless shelter. Was that you?

A   The homeless shelter. So, who's Nancy?

TT   My roommate. She was kinda pissed off that night. Cool. Wow, crazy. Hey guys, I gotta go. Wow. Thanks for the ..draw?

A   Oh, oh, thank you , ah, Teresa ?

TT   Trembley. Okay, thanks you, have a great...

A   Wait. Here, here's my card.

TT   Oh wow, an art dealer. Gee, bye. Have a great evening. *(she exits)*

A   You too Teresa. Good night. Well, well, well, well.

T   It's a great painting Alex.

A   Yes it is.

T   It's haunted.

A   Indeed it is.

T   Deal in the Ditch offered me a grand for it.

A   Deal in the Ditch. A grand. I'm sure I could sell it for eight or ten, maybe even fifteen back east.

T   Fifty-fifty?

A   Thirty-Seventy.

T   Ah Ali, come on... Forty-sixty?

A   What about the babe? The pizza chick.

T   She, she sold it. I'll change something. I was thinking maybe, on the wall over here. A little sketch. An old guy on a horse.

A   Right there?

T   Yeah, not too big.

A   No, not too big. That works. So, what kind is that?

T   Pepperoni, mushrooms, green pepper.

A   Hum, looks good.

T   Yeah, how about you?

A   Veggie, I think, Veggie maybe. What's it say on the slip.

T   Blue cheese drizzle.

A   Blue cheese drizzle? Why not? Give me some of that.

T   Careful man, it's hot.

A   Oh yeah. Umm. Good pizza.

T   Wanta' watch the game? TV's in the living room. I get free cable here.

A   You finally scored a TV, really.

T   It's a big old thing. Rosie gave it to me.
(Alex's phone)

A   What the, oh. Sorry man, I'm gonna take this. Well hello Mary-Ann... I'm just great.... Your husband's out of town,.... Drinkie-poo? Ha, ha. Sure... Your place, yes, of course I know ... Let's say, oh, hour and a half.*(theme music, lights slowly down, sound of the game, continues to talk underneath till black)* Oh yeah I remember... The art thing, oh you know, same old, same... No, no, Mary-Ann, not now, just save till I get there... That's right I'm with a client right now... Yeah. Okay. Okay. Absolutely. Okay.

About the Author

Kempton Dexter, aka Hi-rise Dex, is a compulsive creative. Song-writing, sculpture, public art, painting, musicals, plays and short stories have seduced his attention. His first solo show of paintings was in 1973 while a student at Acadia University. In 1978 in Toronto, besides becoming a father, he trained to eventually become a journeyman wood patternmaker. Arriving in Vancouver in 1984, he helped found Grunt Gallery that same year. Many art shows in the Lower Mainland followed. Since the mid-1990's his focus has been on theatre, music, and writing. Cafes, bars, fringe festivals, and back-yards have been venues for his plays, musicals and songs. His first short story collection, *Mrs. Ceperly's Garden and Other Plots* was published in 2011. His fifth collection of original songs, *Springtime in Vancouver* was released in 2017. *Paris of the Pacific Northwest* is his second book.

Printed in Canada